Uselessness

USE LESS NESS

A Novel

Eduardo Lalo

Translated by Suzanne Jill Levine

The University of Chicago Press

Chicago

EDUARDO LALO is a writer, essayist, video artist, and photographer from Puerto Rico. He is the author of ten Spanish-language books, including *Los países invisibles* and *El deseo del lápiz*. His novel *Simone* won the Rómulo Gallegos Prize in 2013; it was published in English by the University of Chicago Press in 2015. He is a professor at the University of Puerto Rico.

SUZANNE JILL LEVINE is a renowned translator and professor at the University of California, Santa Barbara, where she directs the Translation Studies doctoral program. The general editor of the works of Jorge Luis Borges for Penguin Classics, she is author of the literary biography *Manuel Puig and the Spider Woman*, a work on the poetics of translation, *The Subversive Scribe: Translating Latin American Fiction*, and many translations.

The University of Chicago Press, Chicago 60637
The University of Chicago Press, Ltd., London
© Ediciones Corregidor, 2013
English translation © 2017 by Suzanne Jill Levine
All rights reserved. Published 2017.
La inutilidad first published by Ediciones Callejón, San Juan, 2004.
No part of this book may be used or reproduced in any manner whatsoever without written permission, except in the case of brief quotations in critical articles and reviews. For more information, contact the University of Chicago Press, 1427 E. 60th St., Chicago, IL 60637.
Printed in the United States of America

26 25 24 23 22 21 20 19 18 17   1 2 3 4 5

ISBN-13: 978-0-226-20779-7 (paper)
ISBN-13: 978-0-226-20765-0 (e-book)
DOI: 10.7208/chicago/9780226207650.001.0001

Published by arrangement with Ediciones Corregidor S.A.I.C. y E., Buenos Aires, Argentina.

Library of Congress Cataloging-in-Publication Data

Names: Lalo, Eduardo, 1960– author. | Levine, Suzanne Jill, translator.
Title: Uselessness : a novel / Eduardo Lalo ; translated by Suzanne Jill Levine,
Other titles: Inutilidad. English
Description: Chicago : The University of Chicago Press, 2017.
Identifiers: LCCN 2017021801 | ISBN 9780226207797 (pbk. : alk. paper) |
    ISBN 9780226207650 (ebook)
Classification: LCC PQ7440.L29 I8813 2017 | DDC 863/.64—dc23 LC record available at https://lccn.loc.gov/2017021801

♾ This paper meets the requirements of ANSI/NISO Z39.48-1992 (Permanence of Paper).

The uselessness of lucidity.

Imre Kertész

PARIS

1

There was a time when I could imagine never returning to
San Juan. So many nights, on that walk from the apartment
on Rue de Sèvres—to have dinner with the woman I couldn't
seem to finish separating from, caught up in an uncertain saga
that would take so long to end—I was positive I would remain
in Paris. Paris: contained within its damp, cold walls not only
the traces of men but also the many brilliant words that radi-
ated their stories. I had never experienced anything like this.
It seemed inconceivable I should leave a city that incarnated
such texts.

Marie would wait for me there on the fourth floor; one had
to climb the stairs after crossing the building's inner courtyard. Her studio was larger and more modern than mine, fifteen minutes away on foot, beyond the Boulevard du Montparnasse, on a side street called L'Impasse de l'Astrolabe. I
had lived with Marie my first months in the city, when our
relationship was still a peaceful ritual of habits. There I spent
days reading, using a pocket dictionary and a notebook where
I jotted down the words I didn't know, improving my com-
mand of a language I would grow to love. Just as eagerly, after
what was almost like daily schoolwork, I would go out to ex-
plore the city I had dreamed of, and which now, finally, lay at
my feet.

But by the time this narrative begins, I'd already lost that
world. I'd have dinner with Marie; we'd talk about the same
things we had in the old days, and later, when the sound of the
neighbors' televisions quieted down, we'd move to the bed,
three steps away. But nothing was as before and I rarely slept

there. After midnight, I'd walk back following a slightly different route, heading toward the Boulevard du Montparnasse via a brief stretch of Rue Monsieur-le-Prince, until I got to the corner with my favorite *café-tabac*, delightfully named Au Chien Qui Fume, the Smoking Dog. I'd then cross the avenue and head toward the end of the cul-de-sac, where, on the second floor overlooking the street, I lived in a rundown studio with no heat.

I wouldn't spend the night with Marie because in this sadly calculating way I made my dissatisfaction clear. She didn't seem too bothered by my routine, probably because she didn't want any commitment either. Yet, despite our years of troubled cohabitation and difficult separations—and even with all we did to convince ourselves to the contrary—we were the most important people in each other's lives.

Because I had no contact with anyone from my country during those years, the city started to feel like a kind of desert. Customs I had taken for granted, the ease of routine and long association, were things I didn't have. I didn't have a circle of acquaintances from my native country to share my sense of alienation, my prejudices, or my sense of being in limbo. While I lived in Paris, I was unable to go anywhere without feeling cut off from my own past life.

So, I devised survival strategies. I pursued many passions, but two in particular were with me from the beginning, true symptoms of my situation. Indigenous music and cultures of the Americas: these fascinated me and served to anchor my intellectual life, which, given my Puerto Rican background, was more or less adrift.

After the first few months in Paris, my relationship with Marie deteriorated to the point that we decided to separate for a few weeks. I went to live, for what was going to be a few days and turned into several months, at the apartment of two women friends near the golden dome of Les Invalides. The second week of our separation, I found out that Marie wanted to break up definitively, and to keep me from trying to question this, she announced she had met someone and planned to keep seeing him. I gulped and stupidly acquiesced. We shared so much on a strictly amorous level; but Marie was also my collaborator in reading and writing projects and, as we had lived together in New York, the only person who had known me before I came to France. And besides—I suddenly realized that this was the most excruciating part—she was the only person I could speak Spanish with in Paris. I was losing not only a lover but also my native language. That there were thousands of Spanish speakers in the city didn't matter to me then, because they were all strangers. The pain of being abandoned, which my pride at first couldn't admit to, grew until I found it unbearable.

That night, as I have always done, I took my sadness for a walk. Instead of taking the bus on the boulevard, I wandered around the streets, directionless, confused and wavering under the drizzle, not knowing what to do or what to tell myself. Eventually I made it back to the apartment. My friends had gone to bed. I opened the convertible sofa in the living room, next to Sandrine's big worktable and went to bed without dinner, my hair wet and my body trembling. Oblivious, I didn't care that water had seeped through the neck of my jacket and that my feet were soaking wet. Grief kept me from sleep all night long. Absurdly, at the crack of dawn, I had the thought that I should take advantage of my suffering to go back to writing. And yet only now, after so many years— decades, really—can I bring myself even to recall that night.

The next day, I pretended to be asleep and waited for my friends to make breakfast and leave. Already dressed, I put on my still-wet shoes, grabbed another jacket, and went out for coffee. I walked all along the Champ de Mars and went to sit on the cold steps down to the Seine. Behind me stood the Eiffel Tower, which I had never climbed. Facing me, across the river, was the Trocadéro, the Palais de Chaillot, and my beloved Musée de l'Homme. The morning wasn't excessively cold and I could sit there unprotected from the wind for a while. I had nowhere to go—my friends' house was only a place to spend the night—and I was in no condition to be anywhere I didn't feel at home. I didn't know how to kill time. I had already rejected the idea of going to class at the university that day. I had no one to run to, no one to whom I could pour out my woes. The future stretched before me like a void I couldn't face.

After spending the afternoon out on the street, I walked toward the house where there was the only person I could talk to—absurdly, back to Rue de Sèvres. She welcomed me as if she'd been eagerly awaiting my arrival, exhibiting the ambivalence of dependence versus freedom that undermined our relationship and eventually destroyed it. I had not eaten since lunch the day before and had spent many hours on the streets. When I walked into the apartment that until very recently had been mine, and felt its much-missed warmth and homey atmosphere, I collapsed out of sheer exhaustion. Seconds later, I awoke lying calmly on the rug as if I had slept for hours; looking into Marie's tearful, worried face I asked her—in French, oddly enough, which we never spoke together except for a key word or untranslatable phrase—what was wrong. I had knocked my side against a chair in fainting, and when I stood up, I felt the wrench of pain. We moved to the bed, where, intoxicated by the warmth of the blankets, I fell asleep almost immediately.

I found out later that Marie spent the night with the lights off, sitting beside the only window in the studio, watching raindrops run down the glass pane and the gradual extinguishing of the lights in neighboring apartments. She had taken the phone off the hook to prevent my sleep from being interrupted and to avoid having to confront, at that moment, the cause of her conflicted feelings and our separation. Early the next morning, sitting on a big cushion covered in Polish embroidery, sensing my breathing and her own while she slowly smoked my cigarettes and crushed the butts in a plate we'd used for cheese and crackers, she decided that, even if she didn't want to be with me, she couldn't leave me.

I awoke as it was getting light outside. In the narrow twin bed, I could feel Marie's body beside me. Her long, thick hair flowed over the blankets and on top of my chest. Feeling her breath on my neck, I lay still, thinking, puzzled: what was going on? There was only one bed in the apartment, after all, and Marie had to sleep somewhere.

I got up, trying not to wake her as I made coffee. Two cigarettes were left in the package, so I went out to buy more, and croissants. When I returned, Marie was already up, looking alarmingly serious.

"Do you feel okay?" she spoke as if she had been waiting all night to ask the question.

"Yes, though my hip hurts."

"That's not what I'm asking you," she interrupted. "Last night you fainted. I thought you were dying. You were completely out for almost thirty seconds. *Don't do this to me*. I didn't know what to do. I was about to call SOS Médecins."

I didn't know what to say to her.

"Don't you get it?" she demanded. "Fainting isn't something to take lightly. What happened to you?"

"I already told you, I'm fine. I hadn't eaten for a long time, and I hadn't slept. I don't know, I was very tired and anxious when I got here and I don't remember the rest."

"When you woke up, you spoke to me in French. You didn't have an accent. You can't imagine how it made me feel. It was totally bizarre. You looked so pale, I put my hand under your nose to see if you were breathing, the way they did to Saint Teresa. I was scared out of my mind."

"It's probably nothing. I haven't been feeling well lately, so it makes sense . . ."

"You must see a doctor. I'm going to call my aunt to get the number. We have no idea what's wrong with you. People don't simply faint for no reason."

The supplies I had brought back still lay on the table. Neither of us had made the slightest move to consume them. I picked up the pack of cigarettes. I noticed my half-finished coffee cup and started sipping the cold liquid. For a second we looked at each other. I opened my mouth without knowing what I was about to say.

"Don't speak," Marie said. "None of this is worth killing yourself over. What matters now is that you see a doctor. Stop smoking and eat something. I have to go out now, but you can stay here, if you want. I'll be back later."

She left. She didn't tell me where she was going and I didn't ask. I doubted she was heading for her classes at the university, not today, after what had happened. I imagined she was going to meet her lover. She'd tell him what I'd done, and they'd get embroiled in figuring out some impossible scenario with all three of us still in the picture.

I devoured my croissant and went back to bed. Later I returned to my friends' house and filled my shoulder bag with a change of clothing and a couple of books. When I came back, the apartment was empty. The walls started to close in on me. Nothing had been clarified and I felt more anxious with each hour. I sat imagining what Marie could be doing and pictured only the worst.

My vigil lasted until nightfall. By the time she returned,

Marie had already eaten. She had consulted her aunt and spoken with the doctor who would see us the next day. She said I could stay there that night if I wanted, but it would be better for both of us if I returned to Sandrine and Eve's house. She had thought a lot about us and realized that she did love me, but right now she felt confused. As I knew, she was seeing another man, and she couldn't ask him for more than she could give. Nevertheless, she added, she didn't want to hurt me. We would continue to see each other, although not as often as before, and . . . time would tell.

This speech did not reassure me, but I stayed the night and we made love slowly and conscientiously, as if sex could ever protect us from anything.

I spent many weeks at home with Sandrine and Eve. We became such good friends that their company soon meant as much to me as Marie's. On the weekends they'd leave for the provinces, so for a couple of days I'd have the apartment to myself. Those were the worst. I'd take walks, read, study, go to the movies, but the reality was that I was alone and the hours felt long and difficult. This was when the distance hurt the most. I'd think I was homesick, missing my friends and family, places and expressions that were part of me. But I was really missing Marie.

Those Saturdays and Sundays allowed me to get to know the ordinary, everyday Paris. Workers, bureaucrats, provincial types, the hordes of foreigners invading the streets on Sunday, were all caught up in activities as unsatisfactory as mine. I remember a particular Sunday afternoon when I walked northeast of Les Invalides. The area was residential, and there were few businesses, almost none open that day. It was nearly evening when I entered a very small café, the only one open in that neighborhood. Elderly men were having their aperitif.

I have a vivid memory of the owner who was serving at the bar: He was in his Sunday best in a tie and giant cuff links, as if he had come from a family luncheon. He was in a bad mood, scoffing at the men who came to have a pastis, and was smoking—I don't know why my memory registers this—an English cigarette from a black box. Later, as night fell, I ended up in another café eating the daily special, *steak-frites*. (The steak was probably horsemeat.) I sat next to the window facing the traffic on the avenue, the restaurant almost deserted at that hour, and slowly chewed the tough, barely cooked meat. Painfully, I felt Marie's absence. More than a lover, she had become an old friend who worried about me once in a while, with whom I'd share some food, some comforting words, and a bit of conversation in my language.

The doctor Marie's aunt recommended had been a soldier in Indochina. An old racist, he was, as they say, the total Frenchman. In my emotional state, it didn't take much to worry me, and this physician made it his business to fill me with anxiety. Suddenly my dizzy spell, which had seemed so unimportant to me, led to a place where Illness reigned supreme. He ordered me an infinite number of costly exams and ended up prescribing pills and medications. He diagnosed malnutrition but didn't discard the possibility of a heart condition. I knew I had pushed my body to its limits. I'd thoughtlessly eat whatever came my way. I had all sorts of bad habits, was getting little and poor sleep, and hated the frankly inhospitable weather; so what had happened wasn't really surprising. But my visits to that doctor inspired me to revise my own history into a perfectly neurotic drama featuring, in star roles, fragility and hysteria.

I was overwhelmed. The medication produced such hypersensitivity in my digestion that for a long time I could barely

eat anything without suffering acute gastric pains. Often my
thoughts raced so that I'd clutch my head desperately, not
knowing how to stop my mind, which now focused even more
obsessively on minuscule details. It was almost impossible to
read—or to live, for that matter.

I felt so terrible that I went to visit Marie. After a long talk,
we agreed that she would help me find an apartment. I didn't
like imposing on Sandrine and Eve's hospitality, and besides,
I needed a space of my own. In the days that followed, after
buying newspapers advertising rental properties, Marie and
I went all over the city. We'd put our names on waiting lists
and checked out apartments that always turned out to be
too expensive or far away. We finally found one in pretty bad
shape, but close to Rue de Sèvres, almost equidistant from
the Tour Montparnasse. We ran to the metro to get to the
real estate agent's office before anyone else. The next day,
thanks to a loan from Marie's family and her signature, I had
in my hands the key to a studio on L'Impasse de l'Astrolabe.

Our walks around the city, hunting for a place that would be
mine, brought us closer together and revived the old sense
of common purpose that had first attracted us to each other.
We progressed from a lunch of crêpes in a distant quartier to
an invitation to supper at her house after a walk, to a gleam
in her eyes, which led us to bed. But everything continued to
feel diffuse, unacknowledged and somehow unreal. We had
made love, we had had a good time on the benches along the
Seine or at the movies, but nothing changed. Ironically, our
relationship had become clandestine.

I remember one awful Sunday, the last one I spent in Sandrine and Eve's apartment. As usual, they had left on Saturday morning to go see their families. That afternoon—spring
was already in the air—I was sick and tired of being indoors.

Without any definite plan, I went out to wander around the city. I strolled along the banks of the Seine, stopping at the *bouquiniste* stalls to leaf through secondhand books and look over stacks of old postcards. But I couldn't relax, and I walked for several hours just to try to calm my nerves. I saw how the fleeting joy of Sundays vibrated in the streets and was gradually seized by a visceral fear. I was alone in the vast ocean of that city: between the human beings I saw everywhere and myself yawned an enormous and insurmountable abyss. The move to my new apartment lent a kind of official status to my loneliness. I was afraid that Sandrine, Eve, and Marie would take advantage of it to be more distant. I would remain alone within my four walls, with a world of academic work ahead of me, and an empty life.

When the sun was already setting, I found myself at the Tour Montparnasse. Ceaselessly, the doors of the train station ushered hundreds of people onto the street. The cafés and the restaurants were full, and long lines formed in front of the many movie theaters nearby. Soon, in a couple of days, this would be my neighborhood. I felt a slight and inexplicable change inside me. I could survey the sidewalks in a kind of truce. I stopped to look at everything: movie posters, clothing stores, the Brittany cultural center. I paused in front of a store window with a display of radios and realized that, no matter the little money I had, I would move to the apartment owning one of those. Little by little, I gained a sense of calm. Tired out from many hours of walking, I ventured as far as Les Invalides and circled home. I was finally able to eat something and study a bit for my approaching exams (which I would fail if I didn't buckle down and prepare for in the coming days).

The next day I went to buy a radio. After considering the various models, I chose a relatively expensive one with a cassette player, a shortwave band, and a stereo. I left the store with what felt to me like an enormous box: I hadn't acquired anything this big in many years.

Sandrine and Marie helped me move. I bought a used child's desk from Sandrine's friend and she lent me a mattress that we put on the floor against the bathroom wall. We carried the bed for blocks; to bring the desk over, I ordered a taxi. I went to a store on Rue de Vaugirard near closing time to buy a desk lamp. Then I unpacked the radio and for a long time I used the box it came in as a trash basket. The previous tenant had left a chair.

When night fell, my friends left. Nothing happened as I had imagined it would. In a silence that finally was not oppressive, I felt at ease. I sat down to read, and for the first time in a long time, I experienced the consolation of books. I faced a mountain of pages, but luckily my move coincided with the beginning of the Holy Week recess. I divided my days between the desk and the bed, substituting the book from one course for a book in the other, and even today I remember that week as one of the most pleasurable of my life. Not just because on that table and on that mattress I read the pages of extraordinary books, but because I discovered there the ways in which reading gives meaning to life. The place was as bare as a monk's cell, but I had my thoughts, and my passion for reading. I was alone (especially that week, when all my friends had gone on vacation) but the solitude did not oppress me: I was venturing onto a new path. My moments of rest were spent listening to the radio, an indescribable pleasure.

In those days I came into contact with writers and topics that would change my life. I had to read a long novel by Paul Neptune, which, after a few pages, completely absorbed my days. Along with its literary qualities, the text generated a magical transformation of sorts that showed me a way to connect with the city where I had felt like a stranger. Neptune, playful and brilliant, had taken the map of one Parisian city block and woven together stories about all its inhabitants. Beginning with the social habits of a fragment of the city, he included all classes, the most diverse personalities, professions, tragedies, crises, and accidents. Neptune's narrator brought back to me an experience we have in childhood when we first lose ourselves in a book. The afternoons and nights felt too short for me to read all I wanted of the over six hundred pages of small print in *Rue de Babylone*.

Neptune had just died the year before, when he was still young. This felt like a personal loss: I could no longer meet the man who, through his stories, allowed me to connect with the city I was getting to know on my daily walks.

I soon acquired all his books and even the work he'd published in literary journals. I pieced together his biography: the early death of his parents, his stay in several orphanages, his precocious passion for books and chess. He had not embarked on a university career. Having to support himself, he was prepared to do whatever was necessary. For years he distributed advertisements in the streets, gathered public opinion as a pollster, organized the files of a paleontologist. Finally, when he had established a reputation, he worked for a weekly paper writing a famously eccentric column on chess. His descriptions of the objects on his worktable, gathered in articles much admired by his devoted readers, struck me as miniature sagas comparable, from a certain perspective, to the great novels of the nineteenth century. He was invisible. His country, if he had one, was a modest apartment in a suburb of Paris.

Literature creates imaginary affinities. The sense of connection that sometimes forms between a text, an author, and a reader is one of life's wonders. No reader can forget that moment, just as nobody can forget when he or she finds out that such a connection is only an illusion. My move to that studio was marked by the stories of the inhabitants on that block of a fictional city; from then on, Paris became a world that was an indisputable part of my life.

One of the stories in Neptune's text was about an aborigine, a dark man who lived on the ground floor. Nobody knew where he was from or how he had arrived. The young son of blue-collar workers, who lives in the same building, listens, his ear to the door, to the litanies the man hums at night. His curiosity piqued, on an impulse he doesn't understand, he sets out to learn who the guy is. For days he follows him and finds out that he sings and plays a drum and a bone flute in the passageways of the Maubert-Mutualité metro station and that, every week, inexplicably, he visits some old woman in a bourgeois apartment. Determined to get to the bottom of the mystery, the boy knocks on the woman's door and steps into a world he couldn't have imagined. All the rooms and hallways are filled with indigenous artifacts that come, he will learn, from the Amazon. The woman tells him the story of Klok, the Indian her anthropologist husband, who died a few years earlier, brought to the city, after the man's village had disappeared, devastated by slaughter, disease, and melancholy. Klok, the last warrior of his tribe, was teaching the students at the École des Hauts Études a language whose memory only he possessed and which formed part of a rare family of languages which constituted a kind of lost link in the anthropology of the Tupi-Guarani peoples. He was also a kind of star craftsman for the conservation of feather ornaments, Indian macanas, and bows and arrows in the collections of the Musée de l'Homme.

After the death of her husband, the old lady took care of Klok as best she could. Since his French was rudimentary and nobody, aside from a bookish anthropologist here and there, knew his language, he lived in silence. He dreamed of his lost world, eating frugally, allowing himself the luxury of a pipe, amid rituals and gods who would die with him.

The old woman arranges for Klok to meet the young man and they become friends. They go on excursions together to the Bois de Boulogne and Fontainebleau. Klok collects leaves, bark, and roots. They go to the city parks and run into problems with the police when they climb an old chestnut tree and when, at the Jardin des Plantes zoo, they try to free the falcons. The young man gradually learns Klok's language and religious rites. When Klok catches cold and dies of pneumonia, he takes Klok's drum and sits facing the corpse, chanting accompanied by the old woman in a language that has miraculously survived its last speaker.

This experience will inspire the young man to study anthropology. On his first excursion to the jungle he will carry with him a clay urn with his friend's ashes. His companions will see him get into a canoe and head up river with a handful of Indians. The expedition wasn't supposed to take more than two weeks, but the young anthropologist doesn't return. However, along the tributaries of the Black River, rumors spread about the domain of a white chieftain.

These and other stories by Neptune struck a nerve. When I finished his book, with the sadness of a reader who would have wanted it to go on forever, I was inspired to read more anthropology. I was also taking a course on the indigenous literature of the Americas, which is how I discovered the essays of Pierre Plon, who impressed me so much that I came to read and reread almost all of his work. Like Neptune, Plon had died recently and in the flower of his youth. He had survived many long expeditions to the heart of the jungle, but one morning, as he was crossing the Boulevard Raspail, a milk truck ran him over. He left a brilliant and unfinished body of work that would raise the study of the "savage mind" to new heights. His first book was a heartbreaking chronicle about his fieldwork with a tribe in the Chaco region of western Paraguay. These indigenous peoples had not had contact with the white culture until very recently and would not survive the shock. In the epilogue of his book, Plon told how this society, which he had seen vital and basically whole, had, in the space of five or six years, while he was revising the text, become a little group, disconnected, sickly, in rags, awaiting their end on the margins of the estates of big landowners in Paraguay.

In this and in other more theoretical works, Plon revealed the complexities of a political system that prevented the development of cultural resistance. His findings on the education of children, the difference between the sexes, homosexuality, and the mysticism of these distant beings, opened my eyes to other ways of seeing reality. This broadening of my ideas beyond Western teachings provided me with an invaluable new resource, a way to contemplate life in the city. Plon led me to other books, which led to new volumes and authors. I went to exhibitions, lectures, and films; I spent many hours in the dusty old Musée de l'Homme; I dug up studies and chronicles in the drawers of the *bouquinistes*. Indigenous marginality, the moral status of the defeated, the harsh struggle of indigenous minorities and their earthy wisdom—these became a mythology defining my life in the city. I acquired a series of affectations and practiced them with absolutely serious playfulness. I would buy loose tobacco and roll my own cigarettes; I carried an aboriginal bag on my shoulder; I even bought a Tarahumara drum. I saw myself in the role of the uprooted, the defeated. I embraced and enjoyed this new identity. I pretended to live like Klok and didn't mind that it was all a fantasy.

In spite of all the riches these books brought me, there were times when I couldn't read even one more page. Then I would turn on the radio and lie down in bed. Thus I fell in love with the invisible world coming out of the speakers. For the first time in a long time, I was listening to music with a rich sound, to interviews of artists, filmmakers, addicts or drunken clochards, to stories by authors from all over the world, news, and political scandals. The radio created an intimacy and a state of relaxation that filled me with happiness. Here and there I bought cassettes and built up a library of recordings that did not follow any particular trend: Andean music, Asian and African folklore, French and Latin American songs, ancient music, contemporary and chamber music.

When the holidays were over, I felt like a different person. I had come out of my depression and was enthusiastic about life again. My women friends returned from their family vacations and decided they didn't have to worry about me any more.

I soon learned things weren't going well for Marie. One day she came to my apartment and complained that I hadn't called her—a surprise, given the state of our relationship. She was annoyed and impatient. She had gained weight and was attempting fanatical fasting diets that lasted from six to eight hours, after which, in an uncanny mixture of rapture and defeat, she'd run to the refrigerator or downstairs to the pastry shop to devour whatever she could find. This ambivalence set her nerves on edge. But the primary cause of these manic swings was her love life. The man she was seeing since our separation had not told her he was married. Marie had found out too late—that is, after weeks of bliss—when she was already too emotionally involved with him. I learned from Sandrine that Marie could not tolerate her unknown rival, could not accept that she had been deceived and, in some way, left out of the plot. She'd refuse to sit and talk about it; she preferred to take her anger for long walks.

Just as I had once gone to her, Marie would now come to my apartment to seek comfort. This familiar, impossible situation (crying on the shoulder of her old lover over the love that had split them up) perfectly illustrates the dependency between us and, perhaps, the harsh nature of the city. Paris was a tough place: a sort of an orphanage for lonely adults. Despite their sophistication, few of them seemed able to confront their problems directly. They always found something outside of themselves to blame; they concealed the real source of their distress and their own responsibility behind some big theory. Marie would come to visit me allegedly to discuss one issue—which she then never mentioned—and would remain talking for hours, finding an excuse to stay longer. My reaction was complicated. While I preferred not to see her, I would listen to her for hours, going from boredom and fury to the satisfaction of knowing she was unhappy. I thought that in some way her suffering vindicated me and—though I wouldn't admit it—allowed me to hope we could get back together again.

Whatever it was, I could never have seen what was coming next.

One night, after writing some letters, I realized I still had time to run to Montparnasse and make it to the last showing of a movie. At the ticket office I ran into a French classmate from the university, and we went to sit together. The movie was about an eccentric group of people who founded a utopian community on a small island off the coast of Brittany. It told of the vicissitudes of their idealism that led to a hair-raising dénouement. The head honcho died shortly before a storm, one of their boats capsized, and at the end, the survivors, broken and defeated, decided to return to the civilization they had tried to escape. When the lights came on, Simone and I walked out on the boulevard and chatted until we got to the entrance of the metro. Facing us was a café, and through the windows one could see a group of musicians playing full-tilt boogie. I invited her in and we sat over glasses of beer, trying to communicate over the noise. It was a pleasant and different night. It wasn't easy for a foreigner to meet French people, and Simone captivated me with her openness and good cheer. Past one o'clock, after getting her telephone number, I walked her to the taxi stand, watched her wave good-bye, and headed back to my apartment.

The chat with Simone had filled me with enthusiasm. I decided to take a stroll before returning to the Impasse de l'Astrolabe to prolong the pleasure, the daydreaming the encounter had provoked. When I finally reached my door, I found a puzzling message, written directly on the wood with what appeared to be lipstick. It was a single word, *cabrón* (basically calling me a bastard), traced in separate letters, sloping downward. Incredulous, I read it several times.

At first I thought it might be someone who had tried to get into the wrong apartment. After all, my neighbors were rather rude: I'd had to cover the wall we shared with cork to muffle the racket of their squabbles, glass and dish breaking, and afterwards, the sessions of hysterical and collective bawling. But I decided the insult was addressed to me because it was written in Spanish. I wondered if it could be a joke of Sandrine's, as I had taught her a few words of Spanish. But there was something disturbing in the writing, and in the act itself, which did not fit this theory. After drinking some mint tea and listening to a little music, I decided to forget about it and went to bed.

A knock on the door woke me. Disoriented, I threw on my pants and a sweater and approached the door. I wasn't dreaming. There really was someone on the other side, banging stridently on the wood. I asked who it was and heard Marie's voice. Mystified, I opened the door, and she entered quickly, as if afraid I would block her with my body. I turned around to find her standing in the middle of the studio, looking out of control, as if she were about to attack me.

"Where were you?"

"What do you mean *where* was I?"

"Where were you last night? I came over at nine, at ten, at midnight."

"I was out."

"Out where?"

"Marie, please, what's going on?"

"Where were you last night?"

"I went out. To the movies."

"Who were you with?"

Finally I had a clue. This was a fit of jealousy, out of the blue. For a split second I felt something close to satisfaction, but I also realized that even if that was what it was (and probably it wasn't, or it wasn't only that), there was something inexpressibly sinister about this interrogation.

"I would think that, given the state of our relationship, this shouldn't matter to you."

"Tell me who you were with, who the damn whore was."

The insult was laughable. I would have never imagined it from her mouth, but she said it with an absolutely straight face.

"Calm down, and stop screaming. It's the middle of the night, for Christ's sake. I went out around nine, to the movies, and met up with a friend from the university. After the movie she and I went out for a drink."

"What's her name? Do I know her?"

"What are you after? You're making things up."

"Tell me her name. Tell me her name or I'll start breaking things!"

On my desk next to her were a half-empty wine bottle and an opened notebook. I didn't want to deal with either her hysterics or the mess. I'd lose nothing by giving in.

"Simone."

"Her last name?"

"I don't know it."

"Tell me!"

"Marie, I told you I don't know, and I really don't. Why all this fuss? You go out with other people and I don't ask you anything or persecute you."

"So, you're going out with her."

"I told you that I ran into her at the movies and then we went out to have a beer."

"So, you're going out with her."

"No, and stop already. Sit down."

"I want to know what you were doing with her. I don't want to sit down."

"It doesn't concern you. I don't have to answer. What the fuck is the matter with you?"

Marie was silent and turned her back on me. I could see she was crying so much she was trembling. I went over to her but she whirled around, pushing me away in order to flee. She slammed the door, which had remained opened during the fight, and I listened to her sobbing fade as she ran down the stairs.

I was completely in the dark. I had known Marie for years but had never seen anything remotely like this. She could be impulsive, irrational, and unfair, and I had often been the object of her fits of anger, but the senseless scene that had just occurred was weird and disturbing. I thought and thought but finally went back to bed. Later, assuming the coast was clear, I wiped the door clean. I spent the day uselessly, without concentration or energy, distracted by worry. I hadn't the slightest intention of going to the apartment on Rue de Sèvres to see what was going on, but neither did I want to continue pestering Sandrine with my problems. It was another lonely day.

At ten at night Marie knocked on my door. I opened it; she sat on the bed and began to cry. Interrupted by hiccups, she was weeping softly, which for her was unusual, and begging me to forgive her. She stretched out in bed and asked, with a voice I had a hard time hearing, if she could stay. I remembered my visits to her house a few months ago and thought how impossible it was to overcome fate. I covered her and waited for her to fall asleep before lying down beside her.

When I awoke, I could hear Marie scurrying between the two ranges and the sink, in our excuse for a kitchen. The aroma of coffee flooded the apartment. While I was sleeping, she had gone out to get cheese and bread. The skies were clear this morning, apparently. At breakfast there was no mention of what had happened. I tried to approach the subject with some lighthearted humorous reference, but I saw her change the subject immediately.

I don't know if we fall in love with a person, or with the need for love. I suspect both are true. Marie and I had begun this deaf and dumb dance of blindly groping toward intimacy years earlier. We were united by a passion that coincided with our entry into the adult world. We had assumed (or at least I had) that our relationship was the most solid thing we possessed, but the last few months had proved us wrong. Our separation helped me realize many things. I had lost something, possibly forever. I could no longer naïvely take for granted the meaning of grand words. Here was the unquestionable problem of falling out of love, the human capacity to create suffering. Marie had abandoned me once knowing that I had nowhere to go, knowing that her actions betrayed everything we had said to each other for years. However, she could not erase our history. That last night proved just this. I could imagine her motivations, and what might have happened to her with the man she was after. Who was I for her now? While I provided warmth that had not yet faded away, I was not the being she loved or the one to whom she was committed. We were no longer sharing a life together, nor could we until we could re-create what we had lost. Automatic gestures, affectionate habits, were all that was left, and most probably we both knew this now. Perhaps this seeking of leftovers was why Marie had come to show her desire to be loved, staining my door with an insult. Despite everything I must have been able to see and know in that moment, I stubbornly believed that enduring love was possible. Falling out of love was human, after all, as was our lack of forethought.

That morning, having barely finished breakfast, we made love. This served as an antidote to the bad taste left over from the previous night and all those months. On top of her, in a timeless dimension, I was returning to something that seemed like home. I couldn't or didn't want to admit that sex was a way to avoid talk. We preferred the efficacy of blindness, an intimacy that was really anguish, and loved each other without really knowing the object of our love.

We went out to lunch. We recovered the rhythm of our conversations. We walked around the city bathed by a spring sunlight that accentuated happiness. In a shop, with the concentration and ease with which women pick out clothes for their men, Marie bought a shirt. Then we visited a couple of bookstores. Returning to that place where I could find the things I most cherished, in the company of my female accomplice, was an experience of intense pleasure. I left with books by Neptune and Plon, a novel by Genet, and an illustrated volume of Amazon ethnology. I had no money left and this fact filled me with anxiety as well as joy.

It was starting to get dark later, and at that hour, a little before the stores closed, we bought cheese, bread, wine, and a slice of pâté in a place on Rue de Sèvres. I went with Marie up to an apartment I hadn't seen in weeks. I noticed a few small changes: an old church chair occupied one corner, a shawl covering the bed, in the sink, cups I had never seen, and on the table books I couldn't imagine Marie wanting to read. I suppressed a comment, knowing it would elicit an angry response about my absence. The bed we would share again had been, and perhaps still was, shared with someone. I tried to push that thought aside and to enjoy the supper we enjoyed on the rug Marie's parents had brought from Morocco. But the strain of the day weighed on me, the exhaustion veiling doubts and aggravation over what I was doing. We made love in the mechanical, subdued way Marie tended to do everything, as if she wanted to show me that she was willing to give of herself without asking for anything in return.

We lay there holding each other. Lying face up, I felt her sleeping on my chest. There I was again, beside the woman I loved but whom I had tried so hard to forget. What had just happened, even though I had enjoyed the sex, placed me in a difficult situation. My weakness disgusted me. I was throwing overboard all the work I had done.

I got out of bed and began to dress. Marie opened her eyes and asked what I was doing.

"I'm going home."

"You're not staying."

"I need to be home. It's been a long day. Come see me tomorrow."

"Stay."

"Another day will be better," I said as I bent down to say good-bye.

"You call me."

Marie made it sound like an order. I was too weak and too unwise.

Exams were just around the corner. I was so far behind that, even with the effort made since I had a place of my own, I found myself in desperate straits. I spent the next few days surrounded by books, knowing this was a good excuse to avoid seeing Marie.

When I got back from my first test, I found a note slipped under the door. It was from Sandrine asking me to go see her that night.

I must have suspected that something was going on, because instead of walking over to Les Invalides, I took the bus, cutting short the time it would take to get there. I hugged my two friends (whom I'd barely seen since I had left), realizing I still felt disgust about the time spent in their cold, dark apartment. After chatting about trivialities with Eve, Sandrine took me to her room and closed the door. Marie, whom Sandrine had known since they were teenagers and whom she considered one of her best friends, had come over that morning to accuse her of having gone to bed with me. They had had a shouting match, with insults and recriminations over old injuries that had nothing to do with the present. Confronted with the question of what proof she had, Marie had asserted that I had told her so. Sandrine was beside herself; her friend had convinced her I had lied, and now she attacked me with the intention of unloading all her fury and indignation.

It took a lot of work to calm her down and convince her that Marie was lying. When I lived there, I had ample opportunity to hit on Sandrine and hadn't done so, even when I felt most vulnerable, even knowing that our daily contact had made me like her. Feeling compelled to be sincere, I told her that probably, if she was honest, she had felt the same. We had done many things together and had always had a good time. It wouldn't be surprising if, at some moment, we might have imagined that we could fall in love. Sandrine looked at me with her little blue eyes, nervously twitching the corners of her mouth. I had convinced her, but she tried to keep arguing for a while. She digressed, adding confusion, and while annoyed she also seemed curious or happy about the attraction I had just admitted. I picked up my package of tobacco and rolled cigarettes that were too thin, full of saliva.

We ended up exhausted, with nothing left to say. We lit our cigarettes. She brought over what remained of a bottle of wine.

"I don't know whom to believe," she said.

"You know that I've told the truth."

"Maybe . . . But then why did Marie come to tell me that?"

"I don't know."

"Why did she come to accuse you if you didn't tell her that?"

"I can't explain it, but it's clear that Marie is not well."

"Why isn't it you who's in bad shape?"

I told her all about the last few days, the insult on my door, and briefly, about the rapprochement with Marie. As I told the story, I acknowledged its contradictions, the disturbing gaps along the way. As she listened, Sandrine seemed convinced.

A little later she accompanied me to the door. This time I walked back to my apartment even though it was late and cold, and I had an exam the next day. I would have to get up before dawn to study. I needed to shake off the feeling all this had left me with. It was useless. I arrived home not knowing what to think, and some hours later, in a classroom at the Sorbonne, I did what I could.

I began to dread Marie's visits. I would catch myself making as little noise as possible in the studio, standing absolutely still when I'd hear footsteps on the staircase. I would postpone going home after class, reading in the noisy library at the university, or refueling at a table in a café. It was absurd since Marie was a student like me, and even if I stopped going to classes, she still knew where to find me.

Sometimes I wondered if I should call her. My silence might make her suspect that Sandrine had spoken with me, and given her recent behavior, this could complicate matters even more. I wanted to protect myself by getting away from her problems. This plan was useless because one evening, when I was fed up with wasting time at the Café Universitaire, I took the metro and got off at the station two steps from the Bon

Marché. I had gotten off the stop before hers, so I could think on my way. The store's street stands had been dismantled and the sidewalks finally looked as wide as they actually were. After a few minutes I made it to her building, crossed the familiar courtyard, and went up to the fourth floor. When I had already raised my fist to knock, I heard voices. I stopped short and stepped back when I noticed that one was a man's voice. It was deep and did not sound young. As I had never asked about Marie's lover, I knew nothing about him except that he was married. Any detail, therefore, was news.

Against my better judgment, I pressed my ear to the door. I could barely decipher a sentence here and there. The man spoke slowly, with apparent indifference. Sometimes I could hear the creaking of a chair or the pouring of a liquid. At some point I couldn't stand it any longer. I heard a door open and hurried to descend the stairs, trying not to make a sound with my footsteps. Between the third and second floors, I went faster until I was almost running and just missed bumping into a couple.

On the street I found a café that was just a few steps from the entrance to the house, on the opposite side of the street. I stood at the bar, ordered a beer, and rolled a cigarette with too many loose threads of tobacco on either end. I felt my heart palpitating and my hands trembling as I raised my glass.

For a whole hour, I didn't take my eyes off the door. However, I knew that if the man or Marie came out, I would not approach them. I also knew that if Marie remained alone in the apartment, I would no longer go up there. Ever since the whole story began, I had never been this close to its mystery. These events (Marie being with her lover) were nothing out of the ordinary; the problem was that she had recently come back to me as if none of this existed and, shortly after, had gone to her best friend inventing the story of my betrayal.

When it seemed that nothing was going to happen, and

I was thinking of leaving, I saw the door open. A mature-looking man glanced in both directions as if to get his bearings, and then walked toward the Duroc metro. I left a bill on the counter and did not wait for change. Watching him from the other side of the street, I saw him take a street parallel to the Boulevard Montparnasse, so I crossed and followed him about twenty steps behind. There was no one else on the sidewalk. I saw him stop and search for something in his pockets, next to a car. I continued on and passed him as he was getting into the vehicle. The inside light, which went on when he opened the door, allowed me to see him. He seemed to be about fifty, perhaps a little older; his face had deep lines on his cheeks, his hairline receding in places with gray hair that was carefully combed. He could be anything: businessman, architect, or administrator. His Citroën, without being the most luxurious, was not a modest car. Before the door closed and the light went off, just as I was passing him, I saw, on the back seat, Marie's bag. Now I knew who he was.

One day I heard someone calling me from the street. Sandrine was arriving with a bottle of wine. Her visit, after the bittersweet taste of our last encounter, couldn't help but cheer me up. Far into the night we sat on the worn rug sharing first her bottle and then another bottle we went out to get: making loud toasts and clinking glasses, we laughed our heads off, kicking each other with our bare feet. For dinner I prepared an omelet, while Sandrine looked over the piles of books balanced precariously in a corner of the studio and then she turned the volume of the radio up, perhaps too high. The subject of Marie never came up and I didn't know if it was for the best. On the one hand, I was glad that our friendship left her out of the equation, but on the other hand, I wanted to tell Sandrine what I had witnessed. What was important then was that this visit proved that Sandrine had believed me, and the bottle of wine and her good cheer were an apology for the unfair things she had said to me.

This was the first of many, almost always unexpected, visits. The loneliness I had endured the previous months gradually diminished. One afternoon Sandrine brought, along with some raspberry tarts, news of Marie. She was moving in with her *méc*, or to be more precise, he was moving into her apartment. The news was astonishing. It didn't seem normal that the person I had seen would be willing to live in the reduced confines of the apartment on Rue de Sèvres. We discussed it a bit more but I let the subject drop. I didn't want to admit how much this news hurt me.

I seldom went to class. I spent the days reading texts that almost never had anything to do with my courses. The streets of Paris were always lush with life, and the days turned rapidly into weeks. One night, moved by great determination, I picked up a notebook and wrote the first pages of a story. I returned thus to the calling that had brought me to the city and I spent days writing, enthusiastic and happy. When she'd visit me, I'd tell Sandrine the anecdotes in my stories, seeking in her a substitute for the understanding in these matters I had had with Marie. I'd watch her listening to me with attention and patience, but would suffer when I'd notice a lost look in her eyes. I rarely managed to interest her with the books I'd lend her and the movies I'd take her to see.

At that time, we were a step away from our friendship turning into something more, but the ghost of Marie got in the way. Not even when she invited me to spend a few days at her family home, in a nearby province, did our dealings move beyond spending a beautiful day gathering apples and strolling around the potato fields. At the end of our chats beside the fireplace in the large kitchen, there were a few good-night kisses and each to his or her room with lots of questions in our minds.

One day, at the university, I ran into Simone, who still felt familiar from that night when we'd seen a film together and then shouted at each other over loud music. She was a big smoker, with yellow stains on her fingers. She lived with her father, a disabled war veteran. Her mother, who couldn't get over what had happened during the Occupation, had hung herself when Simone was seven. The wounds left by the family history could be seen in her impulsive behavior, her constant smoking, and her way, at the slightest provocation, of pressing her body against mine. Without meaning to, I felt her hips bump against me when we walked along the sidewalks or got up from a table in a café. It was impossible to walk in a straight line. I was tempted, but held back because Marie, despite everything, was still a part of me.

I don't know how many opportunities I missed out on because, in my loneliness, I still wanted her, a desire that in the long run led nowhere. I kept waiting for something to happen, and assuming that I still had a role to play in the drama of Marie's life. Despite the reality, clear as the nose on my face, I went on being faithful.

2

32 The uncertainty became unbearable. One day I couldn't restrain myself and walked over to Rue de Sèvres, after calling
Marie to let her know I was coming. When the door opened,
I thought for a moment I had knocked on the wrong one. She
had cut her hair above the shoulders and was now a redhead.
She had gained weight and was wearing a suit, something she
never wore.

For a few awkward minutes, I was at a loss. Was this the
woman I'd shared my life with for years? Was this Marie, my
soul mate, now apparently disguised? Losing all confidence,
I regretted coming. Stalling, I asked her for a drink so that I
could watch her walk away.

She was bringing a glass over to me when we both heard
someone coming up the stairs and she froze in terror.

"Hide in the bathroom," she whispered.

"You can't be serious?" Her request was totally out of line. I'd
rather witness a scene (which, after all, would be between her
and her friend, and the internal politics of their relationship
did not concern me) than place myself in a stressful situation
that was undignified and—if the man were violent and para-
noid, which could be inferred from Marie's fear—dangerous.
We heard the footsteps reach the fourth-floor landing. Marie
stared at the door intensely, as if it were a hallucination. Finally we realized the footsteps had announced her neighbor's
arrival.

"Marcel is jealous," she said, trying to explain her behavior.

"You don't say?" I didn't hide my sarcasm.

"Don't make fun of me."

"I'm not. It's just that I've seen you doing something I could never have imagined. Don't you get it? I don't care if you believe me or not, but I never thought you would stoop to this."

"To what?"

"I have to explain?"

"I have a relationship with another man and he's not you. There's no reason for you to get involved."

"I'm not getting involved, and you're right, it's not my problem. But I wasn't the one who wrote *cabrón* on my door, who almost broke the door down and then went off without explaining what the hell's the matter. You're the one who then comes back and goes to bed with me and says she loves me, and begs me to forgive her, and that I have to understand."

"I never asked you to forgive me! I have nothing to apologize for!"

"I suppose, then, that your behavior is normal and natural. Coming and going and tearing off your clothes is the same thing as shaking hands or going to the movies one night."

"I was having a rough time. If I explained it to you, you'd understand. Besides, one thing has nothing to do with the other. This stuff happens. Maybe not to you, but certainly to most people."

"Don't be stupid. Do you happen to have statistics about these things? Is your terror a moment ago normal? Is it normal to do what you've done to me knowing that I had nobody in Paris, or any place to live?"

"The apartment you have is in my name. You got it thanks to me."

"That's true, but thanks to you I lost everything too. Besides, it doesn't matter now. What matters to me is to know what game you're playing—I can't call it anything else—what your intentions are, why so stupid and cruel."

She went to the bathroom. Through the door I heard her crying. I waited a while before going in. She sat on the toilet, her face in her hands. She reached out to me. I lifted her up into my arms and held her as she cried. She blew her nose with pieces of toilet paper, a few sticking to her nose, and went to lie down on her bed. I sat next to her.

"I don't know what's wrong with me. The days go by, and it's as if I weren't living. I'm afraid. I'm afraid everything will get worse."

"What?"

"Life, my life, I can't tell you exactly. Marcel is married. He has three daughters. I've met them: the oldest is at the university. She's almost my age. He told me he was going to leave his wife, that he would come live with me, but he didn't stay more than a weekend. He lies to me and I'm afraid. He sells jewelry and has a gun. But that wasn't why I asked you to hide. That's not why I'm afraid."

"Why, then?"

She took some time to answer.

"I love him. He's not easy, but I love him. I always want to be with him. I can't get him out of my system."

I wasn't the right person to be listening to these confessions, and yet I knew I was the only one Marie could confide in. What would endure above and beyond all else, including that man, was what we had meant and continued to mean to one another.

"I can't go on like this." I didn't understand. She seemed to jump from one topic to another. "I have pains, here in my chest. Sometimes I can't breathe and I see black at the sides of my eyes, as if I were going blind, as if some awful, strange thing were about to happen to me. Besides, there are the bugs, the bugs that get into my skin."

I was completely lost.

"They come at night and don't let me sleep. They get into my eyes, nose, anus, and vagina. They're so little that you can barely see them, but I feel them. I try to crush them but they move too quickly. I know that it sounds like a dream, but it isn't a dream. They move around inside me, I feel them rubbing their antennae, going from place to place. They eat in my veins. They buzz all the time."

Marie stood, gazing at the ceiling. She didn't blink.

"Marcel says I'm crazy. But he doesn't know what's happening to me. He says it's nothing."

"What are you talking about? What bugs?"

"They buzz in my head. You can't imagine, it's like a plague of locusts. Remember that movie we saw about the wheat fields on the Great Plains? Something like that."

"You're hallucinating."

"No."

"We have to find out what doctor to go to; I'll go with you if you want."

Marie stood still.

"Go. He'll be here any minute."

Again I felt my neediness. Even with all the distance that lay between Marie and myself, she continued to matter more to me than anyone else in the city. I had nothing to fill her absence with, no one to replace her. She lived so nearby. I had tried to forget her but still felt drawn to what she had been for me. Her ravings upset me and filled me with ambivalence. I wanted to be with her, but at the same time, I wanted to run away.

I called the next day.

"I hope you're feeling better."

"I am," she answered with doubt in her voice.

"Really?"

"You must forgive me for what happened yesterday. Sometimes I can't think in a straight line. Please also forgive me for the other thing. I'll get over it."

"What's the other thing?" I asked.

"The bugs," her voice had faded to a whisper. This wasn't the answer I was expecting. "Don't take me seriously. These are things that not even I understand. It's crazy, I know, but very real at times. More real than what I see with my eyes opened. Forgive me if I've hurt you and if I still am hurting you. I don't know if it means anything to you to hear this, but I love you, I love you very much and I'll always love you."

"And I love you."

We were silent.

"Marie," I said, "What's happened to us?"

"I don't know," I felt her on the verge of tears.

"I've never understood."

"Perhaps there's nothing to understand."

"But something must have happened. Something I've done or said."

"It wasn't you or me. It was something that was in our path, something that even setting our mind to we couldn't have avoided. Some things have to happen and make no sense. Don't waste your time."

There was a pause before she spoke again.

"I don't want to lose you."

I didn't know what was in those words, whether it was remorse or a request, or if they were a formula to express the pain of separation or some other incalculable series of emotions. They were, anyway, words I really couldn't answer, no matter what I said.

"Me neither," I said.

"Whatever happens, you'll always be with me," Marie was crying. It was yet another of her crying jags I had experienced so often.

"That's why I can't understand what's happened to us, and what's happening to you," and I added, "Why don't we give each other another chance? Why don't we begin again?"

"If Marcel weren't in the middle, that would be okay."

Nothing made sense. I had crossed the line that I had promised myself, in my more lucid moments, I would not cross. I didn't have time to think it through, and I was, myself, afraid of being alone. The telephone seemed like a fragile, inadequate connection.

"He doesn't have to be in the middle. That's in your hands."

"But I can't break with him now. I love him."

"You love him, or you're afraid of him?"

"Both, perhaps. It's all the same."

"You can't love someone and fear them at the same time." I opted for truisms, for the reasoning of common sense. But I still knew that what Marie was saying was not only possible but also probably true. I was being stupid.

"I don't know. The problem is I can't figure it out, I can't go one way or the other."

I couldn't back off. The conversation itself compelled me. I had to fight until I convinced her.

"But you have to do something, because in this situation nobody is okay and it's not fair to anyone. Not even to yourself."

"I can't decide now even if I want to."

"You've got to do it."

"I don't want to talk anymore."

My days revolved around a single objective. I was drawn to her in the same way I would sometimes finish smoking a cigarette simply because it was lit, acting out of anxiety.

I would call Marie, and we'd see each other frequently, reproducing almost infinite variations on that phone conversation. I could see the signs of her deterioration. Gradually, imperceptibly, a gesture she made with her mouth acquired the aberrant rhythm of a tic. Her hair had not been colored again, exposing a commingling of colors. Marie would incessantly twine it around her fingers, making braids, pulling it, untwining it, and little by little, she created a bald spot on the top of her head. She'd go without eating, and then, dying of hunger, she'd fill herself with anything within reach: desserts, cheese, sausages, the remains of old, stale food from dinner.

Summer and the season of final exams were approaching. I shut myself in to study. I'd punctuate my work with dinners beside the radio. I'd listen to interesting programs: roundtables of film or theater critics, which turned into spectacular battles, long and irreverent interviews with all sorts of individuals, world music which I would then seek out in the cassette sections of stores. It was edifying and kept me company, putting on the back burner the pain in my back and in my soul.

One evening, when I came home after finishing a four-hour exam, I decided on a whim to stop by Marie's apartment. I wanted to go out with her to eat crêpes, to take a walk as a break from my study routine. I could go to her house without calling in advance because we had agreed upon a system of signals. If Marcel were visiting her, the bathroom window would be open. I peeked into the courtyard and checked that she was alone. As soon as she let me in, I realized something was up. She had a suitcase on the bed and was filling it; she wouldn't look at me.

"You're going somewhere?" I asked, feigning naïveté.

"Yes, tonight."

"Where?"

"Marcel has a business trip and maybe, afterwards, a few days of vacation. I didn't tell you before because I've just found out."

The lie and her pretense that I shouldn't be upset infuriated me.

"I came to find out if you wanted to have dinner with me," I said, humiliated, controlling the violence that I didn't allow myself to express.

"I'm soooo sorry," she dragged the sounds, with silly gestures, "but I can't now."

"I can see that you're still in your world."

She didn't turn to look at me, but I knew she was alert, sensing that something was about to happen, that her little comedy act had been a mistake.

"Missus number two is going on a trip."

"Don't talk like that."

"She will enjoy fly-by-night hotels near train stations. Oh, the delicious dinners in the Bistros de la Gare!"

"It's more than you can give me."

"But you don't realize that you're not getting anything out of it."

Finally she looked at me. She didn't know what to say, but she would attack anyway. The point was to wound and to win.

"What do you know about what he gives me? You have no idea what passion is. I was with you for so many years and I couldn't do it anymore. Out there, in the real world, there are other people and they're not like you. Poverty gets old and you do too. Finally I was fed up. Let's see if you finally realize now. I'd better shut up because I don't want to hurt you." She accused me of being cold, but my blindness, my stubborn pursuit of Marie above and beyond all reason, were anything but cold. I too was fed up with myself, with her.

"Fine, we won't see each other anymore," I said and it was only when my words came out that I was aware of the clean break they proposed. I couldn't stop there. One sentence led to another: "Be alone then, or with him or whomever you want. I don't care. *Bon voyage.*"

I stood up and, for the first time since I'd arrived, we were facing each other, feeling a surprising desire to embrace. We looked at each other expectantly.

"Good-bye," I said.

Marie spoke from the threshold, as I was already going down the stairs.

"I'm sorry. See you soon."

I remembered certain texts by Neptune, written at a table in a café near the Alésia metro station, which recorded his meticulous observations over a period of several days. With its statistics of misery the city was there in all its entirety.

My attraction to Simone—with whom I took an exam and went out frequently during that time—was no coincidence. She introduced me to places and people I otherwise probably would never have known. We went to tiny bars with minimal decor where the local customers drank countless glasses of red wine, enveloped in the thick smoke of Gitanes cigarettes. At the tables sat workers with oozing sores on their hands and lonely, bitter women who had a tender word only for the dogs they treated as their children. I'll never forget the parties at the house of Simone's cousins. When her aunt, a fat woman around seventy years old and eccentrically wrapped in two multicolor shawls, opened the door to us the first time, she gave her niece big kisses and, without a greeting or handshake, immediately gave me the generous glass of whiskey she had in her hand. The ancient apartment, with its many small rooms, was always dark, as scarves or handkerchiefs were draped over almost every lampshade. In one corner of the living room there was a Rouault, since, despite appearances, her aunt was well educated, a staunch disciple of Jacques Maritain, and Catholic. Her offspring were an extraordinary collection of eccentrics. The eldest, who was a professor of architecture and also had a PhD in philosophy, barely spoke, and drank one whiskey after another in a corner of the library while reading a novel by Simenon. Her oldest daughter had been in analysis for over ten years: she had twice attempted

USELESSNESS   41

suicide, was a kindergarten teacher and a fanatical reader of Marguerite Duras. However, the most interesting thing about her was that her daughter's father had been her own mother's student and lover. Another daughter was no longer a daughter but a son who, after many trips to Holland, had completed a sex change. Sometimes he'd show up at these soirées with his girlfriend, a rather overweight blonde who worked at a post office. The youngest, closest to Simone, had converted, successively, to Hinduism and to Islam, and then after spending some time in Fez, had just returned to France and had rather fanatically rejoined the Catholic fold. If they had enough to drink, they were the perfect family. Gradually they'd all flop onto the sofas and the beds, twisting in contortions, uttering incredible words or calling attention to themselves in hilarious ways. At the end nobody would say good night. If you wanted to go, you would simply open the door and leave.

Simone and I would leave the apartment laughing hysterically, seriously drunk, amused by our zigzagging footsteps. Our rides on the last metro seemed endless because the motion made us dizzy. On more than one occasion, I had to take Simone home and hold her head over the toilet. Afterwards, she'd flop onto the mattress and go straight to sleep deeply until late morning. Later, she'd make some vague excuses, and with a cup of coffee and the first cigarettes of the day, we'd recall the collective delirium staged by her relatives.

Despite these festivities, I still couldn't find my way out of this dark period. When I was by myself, as I usually was, I tried to soften the tedium by drinking wine before going to bed. Often this meant I'd stay up until dawn beside the radio, rolling a cigarette between sips, feeling the early hours were the best time of the day. Then, after so little sleep, I'd spend the day tired, feeling out of sorts. I'd find some consolation in my routine activities, but there was always, deep down, the unsteadiness of what I had lived in the city and that, now, after the last incidents with Marie, had intensified.

I had only a vague idea of what I really felt. I experienced everything through the opaque filter of a love story. Love was the big catchall of all my problems, a big dictionary of false definitions.

Sandrine brought the news. Marie had attempted suicide and was in the hospital. The story we were able to piece together that night had a lot of holes. Some time later we learned she had sunk so low that Marcel had no choice but to reduce his visits and invitations to her. Apparently Marie had demanded that he leave his wife. She didn't realize that was impossible.

She spent days without leaving the house, using up the last of her food, calling her lover's office every hour, and at night, calling anyone listed in the telephone book. Finally, she decided to swallow a whole bottle of antihistamines. Then, sleepy and nauseous, tormented by her failed attempt, she had slashed her left wrist with a kitchen knife. The pain and blood forced her to react. She called her mother in New York, who, terrified, immediately telephoned the Paris police. When the policemen arrived at Rue de Sèvres, they found her sleeping with the door opened, a kitchen rag tied around her left hand, and upon being awakened, sufficiently lucid to tell them what had happened. Fortunately the wound had not been deep and had not reached her veins. Because the police were involved, she couldn't leave the hospital until they had done a psychiatric evaluation. Her mother had landed in Paris that afternoon and called Sandrine. She invited us, Sandrine and me, out to dinner the next day.

I had to cut short my study hours to go see Marie in the middle of the afternoon. The hospital was far away, outside of the Paris municipal jurisdiction, in one of the peripheral suburbs. I got off at the last station of the metro line and entered through imposing doors. One had to walk a long ways to the hospital pavilions. After asking at several counters, I located her room. I was seeing her for the first time in several weeks and expected a dramatic change. When I came in, I found her sleeping. Her face was pale but amazingly peaceful. An intravenous line was connected to her right arm, and on her left hand and wrist was a bandage with a dark bloodstain.

I couldn't stand the atmosphere. For the first time, the seriousness of the act she had committed was clearly evident. I fled to the inner courtyards seeking air and found steps to sit on, beside a pillar in the shape of a lion. The day was cold and cloudy, matching my mood. I thought how it was like so many days in Paris. Here death was dark and clammy, very different from the way it was under the sun of the tropics. I went to a lounge with dark, stained walls to get a big cup of café au lait. I smoked slowly, having to light the cigarettes I rolled again. The dirt on the walls, the voices of the nurses, the melancholy, the linear coldness of the garden, Marie's deceptively peaceful face, her calm and breathing body, the body she had wanted to deprive of life—all seemed unreal to me. I spent some hours there, sipping a coffee that had arrived lukewarm and had been ice cold for a while. I couldn't make sense out of what was happening. I was simply there, witnessing events that went beyond me.

When I got back to the room, she was awake. They had brought her a tray of food; it was on a table next to the bed. Upon seeing me, she turned her eyes away ever so slightly, conveying more desolation than she could have with any other gesture. I sat in the only chair and realized I hadn't brought her anything—not flowers or fruit or even a book. Empty-handed, I didn't know what to say, how to take in that look that was lost somewhere on some point in the wall.

I went to speak, but Marie lifted a finger and put it in front of her lips. Down her cheeks rolled two tears.

The rest of the afternoon was horrendous. Marie's mother arrived after a while with huge bouquets of flowers, complaining that she couldn't open the window adequately to air out the room. She began to dash to and fro in her usual overbearing way without taking into account that the room was so silent that you could hear a pin drop. She gave me a significantly slow greeting, with a short and intense look that indicated that afterwards we needed to talk. We had never liked each other. She had very clear ideas about what her daughter should be and do. In New York she would arrange dinners where there were always a couple of eligible Frenchmen among the guests to serve as bait. Her insidious violation of all personal boundaries had failed, and the only thing she accomplished was to make Marie suffer. When push came to shove, her mother and I had managed to put up with each other, but I knew that if she'd been able to, she would have eliminated me from the scene long ago.

I witnessed her overwhelming chatter, which never managed to include Marie beyond a monosyllable and a few furious *no*s. She insisted on pretending that everything was perfectly fine, and that her daughter, instead of trying to kill herself, had twisted her ankle. I looked at my watch, calculating how much longer the torture would continue and wondering where Sandrine was.

It was a relief to see her in the doorway. She was bringing another bouquet of flowers. Marie's mother greeted her with an effusiveness that felt false. Her social poise consisted of this: she could seduce with a smile and good manners, keeping to herself, for later, the judgments she would act upon. After a few minutes, Sandrine gave me a look behind the mother's back, invoking my complicity. The grand lady couldn't hide her discomfort. In her world people didn't commit suicide, period. There was a certain pleasure in imagining the versions of the facts she would invent on both sides of the Atlantic.

Finally, when loudspeakers announced the end of visiting hours, we could look forward to a change of scene. Even then, Marie's mother detained us at the door for a few more minutes, insistent upon arranging the improvised flower vases, asking her daughter about minute details, and going over to cover her and giving the room a once-over as if it were a dining room before the arrival of guests. Outside, Sandrine offered me a cigarette so I wouldn't have to roll one in front of the mother, who I am sure would have added this habit to the long list of my defects.

A taxi took us back to the city. Her mother had made a reservation in a restaurant on a street near the arcades of Rue de Rivoli. The moment we arrived I realized I was not dressed appropriately. My budget did not allow for visits to this kind of establishment. And besides, I didn't feel comfortable with the subservient pomp and ceremony of the waiters, which mimicked in its fashion the practices of the ancien régime. The immense menu had, inside its leather covers, paper with an intricate and elegant typographical design. I ordered one of the few dishes I recognized, filet of cod, which came covered with a thick sauce and a salad that was supposed to be delicious. The mother, whose husband shared her tendency toward conspicuous consumption, did not even suggest the house wine.

It took time to get to the point. Sandrine and I listlessly answered questions about our work or studies, recent vacations, family, or the future. We saw how she let the dinner drag on, peering over our heads at the other diners and playing with the crust of the bread. We had to wait, according to her elegant protocol, for the arrival of the desserts in order to mention Marie.

She began by saying that we had to understand the worries of a mother. What had happened could not be taken lightly, and she was ready to exercise her natural right. Marie had not explained anything concrete, had not offered any cause, and therefore, her mother had to resort to us as sources. If this didn't work, she would have no other choice but to go to the authorities in order to initiate an investigation. Like an imperial ambassador, she was delivering her ultimatum. Either we collaborated with her, violating all loyalty to Marie, or we would have to face the police.

I attempted one last strategy I thought might work.

"We cannot know, madame, what you yourself do not know either."

"But what is this? You're my daughter's boyfriend. You doubtlessly must have seen some sign, some display of fragility." She always addressed me formally as *vous* to make it amply clear that I didn't belong in her circle.

"Not anymore. We broke up months ago."

"You don't say?" She received the news with equal doses of suspicion and satisfaction.

"Well, this must have something to do with it. Tell me, what was the nature of the breakup?"

"I wasn't the one who wanted to break up. It was Marie."

"*Ah, bon.* How's that for news? My daughter never tells me anything."

"That's the truth," Sandrine intervened. "During the crisis, he spent several weeks in my house."

"What happened then? What was the crisis?"

"A breakup is always painful," said Sandrine. "I know that Marie loved him and was sad, a bit depressed then, but it wasn't anything unreasonable or unnatural. After all, she wanted to end the relationship. She wanted to spend some time alone."

"I don't understand," said her mother. "Why did they separate?"

"I don't totally understand it either," I said. "As I've said, I'm not the one who wanted to part."

"But really, tell me, why does someone take a kitchen knife and cut her wrist? You can't imagine how her voice sounded on the phone, the horror I lived, how helpless I felt being so far away. What you're saying doesn't explain anything. Either you're idiots or you are lousy friends."

"Madame, we cannot be responsible for Marie's actions. Even though I didn't want to stop seeing her, I accepted what she wanted, went to live at Sandrine and Eve's house, and then got my own apartment. Obviously I didn't see much of your daughter after that time, and when I did, it wasn't in the same way as before, for reasons you can easily understand."

"What you're saying is that you abandoned her."

"Madame, for God's sake, that's ridiculous."

"One is loyal to one's friends, forever."

"And so I've been, but Marie wouldn't have accepted such supervision. I was her partner, not her father."

The sorbets had melted. Silently we ate spoonfuls of the delicious, sugary liquid. She offered no coffee or herbal tea but rather signaled the waiter to bring the bill. Marie's mother didn't want us to accompany her to the hotel. She hailed a taxi and gave the driver an address less than two minutes away. She said good-bye, shook my hand (I was no longer anything to Marie; she didn't have to continue pretending to be affectionate), and kissed Sandrine, bending her torso forward to separate her body as much as possible from hers.

We walked as far as Châtelet, relaxed in each other's company after so many uncomfortable hours. We sat in one of the cafés in the plaza. Warm weather already allowed for the permanent installation of tables on the sidewalk. The visit to Marie followed by that awful dinner with the mother had left us exhausted, no energy left even to talk about it. We sipped our beers observing the tourists who had begun to invade the city in droves. From time to time we exchanged a comment, something ironic about the mother, which made us smile. We mentioned Marie only a few times, conscious of the fact that we shouldn't say anything further for the moment, that neither of us really wanted to reveal what we were thinking.

We assumed the mother's threat would not be carried out. Marie was more of a concern. Now, far away in the hospital room, she could be lying wide-eyed, reliving a sort of hellish rerun of her crisis. The bits of information we had were not enough to help us understand. My mind kept replaying our evening with the mother. I told Sandrine this, as she raised to her lips the glass of beer, without presuming she'd understand, without wanting to explain.

A little later, dog tired, we walked to the taxi station. We agreed to meet at the hospital the next day.

So began the drama that would last for weeks and that, in the end, would never really be resolved. Marie didn't speak, didn't eat, and even urinated and defecated in bed. Visits were unbearable. Her body lay, as if all the rest of her was absent, almost always on its side, facing the wall or the night table, with the room submerged in the nauseating smell of the bouquets the mother would bring every day. Sometimes, sitting in the chair, waiting for visiting hours to pass, I would realize that she was looking at me. This would make me shift my position. I didn't know what to do except to take her hand, always lifeless. Later, I'd have the ten minutes walk to the metro, the long trip changing trains, dinner at any old café, and the uselessness of sitting as time passed in my room. Sometimes I tried to forget her with the radio, my books, or with the one or two letters I'd rarely carry to the post office.

I had taken the last exam of that summer session, but I was not planning to return to my country. I wanted to spend the summer in the city and to save my family the cost of the trip.

Independently of whether my presence would be helpful, I also reasoned that I shouldn't leave Marie alone. Besides, ever since I had moved to the apartment on the Impasse de l'Astrolabe, the city had become my home. It was no longer an alien landscape.

My birthday was coming up and I decided to organize a dinner at home. Sandrine, Simone, Eve, Sylvie, the religious pioneer who was Simone's cousin, and Hamed, her Moroccan boyfriend, told me they would come.

On the afternoon of the day of the celebration, I went by the hospital a little earlier than usual. Nothing had changed. It was the same silent routine. At the end of the hour I went over to her to say good-bye. When I was going toward the door, I heard a word that sounded like an explosion in that world of shadows.

"Happy birthday."

I turned around so surprised that Marie couldn't keep from smiling.

"Yes, I still know how to speak. I also know what day it is, but don't tell anyone."

I hugged her with emotion, with a joy I have seldom felt.

"You're better. You're going to get well?"

"We'll see. Go now and have a nice day. Make sure to come back when Mom isn't here and I promise you we'll talk."

"You know I love you."

"Believe me, I know."

"Your voice has been the best gift."

"Thank you. Go now."

"Till tomorrow then."

"Yes, till tomorrow. Don't go falling in love tonight."

It was like I was walking on air to the metro. Uplifted by her voice, I felt a bright burst of energy. That night, in a city where I had suffered so much, I enjoyed the luxury of happiness. At my party gifts were heaped upon me (Simone brought seven, they were playful silly things: a bag of marbles, four or five stamps, a packet of Gauloises without filters, a roll of North American toilet paper). The guests missed the last metro and took a taxi to spend the night at Sandrine and Eve's place, since it could accommodate them. Before going to bed, I had a last glass of wine, enjoying the cool night air coming in the window, which I could finally leave open.

The next day, I went to the hospital. In my pocket I had Neptune's novel to lend to Marie. As I didn't want to run into the mother, I decided to spend a little time in a café after I got out of the metro. The city was dressed in its summer best. Few things could compare with the pleasure of a European season when everything vibrates, bathed in a rich yellow light. After a half hour or so, with real anticipation, I entered the great doors and walked to the hospital pavilions. When I reached the corridor where Marie's room was, I realized that one of the male nurses was looking at me strangely. I went to the door, knocked and entered. The bed was empty and her stuff had disappeared. On the floor were petals and leaves that had fallen as the room had been emptied.

I went over to the counter of the nursing station to ask.

"They transferred her this morning, monsieur."

"Where? To another hospital?"

"We can't tell you. You would have to speak to the doctor or the family."

"Where do they transfer cases like this? To which hospital in the city?"

"I've told you that we are not allowed to give out that information. Besides, usually they are not transferred: they are usually discharged, or locked up."

"And was she locked up?"

"I told you, she was transferred."

I went back to the café and looked up the telephone number of the hotel where her mother was staying. They told me she had left that morning. Then I took the metro to Invalides. There was no one at Sandrine's apartment. I killed time in a park before going back and finding that she had not returned. Then the only thing I could think of doing was to walk over to the steps of the Seine, to the place where, months before, I had felt the weight of my misery. The season now made the area less lonely. A woman had set up her easel next to the wall and was painting river barges; a few couples were amusing themselves on the benches; an elderly couple was walking along the river's edge. The afternoon was extraordinarily beautiful, but my delight in it had vanished. I smoked without pleasure, my mouth feeling irritated and dirty.

I knew Marie's mother wouldn't have the decency to let me know what she had done with her daughter. She could always use the excuse that she had no way to call me. I was hoping that she might be more bighearted with Sandrine.

When I returned to the apartment, Sandrine had just arrived. I told her what had happened and she was puzzled. She hadn't heard anything either, but she did have, in her address book, the number of Marie's aunt.

She dialed immediately. Besides the usual microphone and receiver, French telephones have a little handpiece for a third party to listen in on the conversation without participating. I had always found this idiosyncratic form of espionage surprising. Armed for the first time with this prop, I listened in on the conversation.

The aunt was following a script. Her cordiality and surprise were too cloying. She promised to find out what had happened and to call us as soon as possible. We waited almost two hours before dialing the number again. We listened to her evasions until Sandrine forced her to say more by pretending to be worried to death. The mother had managed to throw her weight around enough to have Marie declared mentally incompetent. At that moment, they were on their way to

New York, where a room for Marie was reserved at a psychiatric hospital. She didn't know which one, but she was sure it
was the best. Her sister treated her daughter like a queen. She
either didn't know or couldn't say anything more. She ended
by insisting that Sandrine never let anyone know that this
conversation had happened.

"But madame, why didn't she let us know?"

"Well, there were more important things to do."

"At the very least, it's not right."

"What can I say? My poor sister is going through hell."

"But we are Marie's friends and we were always with her. We
have a right to know, at least to be notified."

"I have nothing to do with this, but my sister must have her
reasons. The two of you, though I understand your situation,
are in no position to make demands."

She quickly said good-bye and hung up.

Sandrine pushed the phone away, cursing at her. She suggested a few courses of action to me but knew we could do
nothing. Marie had vanished. Someday, when she could escape
her mother's clutches, we would have news of her again. Now
it was clear that we had lost her. It was all over now, no extenu-
ating circumstances, no hopes. All this had actually happened
quite a while ago, but the occasional contact with her, not to
mention my pain, had kept me from accepting, digesting, or
getting over it. I recognized once again the grip of loneliness,
the void in which Marie (even the distant, crazy Marie) was
leaving me. I dined joylessly with Sandrine. Then I walked
home feeling certain that for the first time I was truly alone.

3

With summer, Paris came to life again, but all the bustling felt alien, part of the lives of others. I remained, in my head, on this side of the Atlantic, with a sensation of anxiety and depression that never left me, not knowing how to fill my days. I thought both of returning and not returning to Puerto Rico. The idea of another year in this state crushed my energy, which was already diminished by Marie's disappearance. I couldn't get her suffering out of my mind, or the foundation of the bridge that she had begun to build toward me the day of our last encounter.

I ended up telling the whole story to Simone. One Sunday we went for a walk along the islands on the Seine and stopped to sit on a bench facing Notre Dame. My tale took up over an hour, and even though our relationship hadn't felt intimate until that moment, I didn't find in her the indifference of ready-made answers. Finally she said that I seemed so fragile that she was afraid to touch me.

We started seeing each other more often. We'd go to the movies, chasing down in distant quartiers reruns of old movies, which a certain sector of the public had not forgotten. We'd go to Sylvie and Hamed's apartment in the Tenth to have dinner; we'd sit down to chat beside the ponds and along the promenades in the Jardin du Luxembourg. She was right: I could have collapsed at any moment. I felt I was living in a void, and what I perhaps didn't want to admit to myself was that I dreaded what could happen between us. I'd watch her reclining on a chair with her eyes closed and her skirt raised to get some sun on her legs after winter, and I endlessly went back over my doubts. In spite of a certain grace, Simone wasn't a beautiful woman, but I was fascinated by her inexhaustible energy and deep roots in the city, her universe of tastes and tendencies, so different from my own, and yet I held back, which, I hoped, wouldn't offend her.

Absurdly it was hard to watch her trying to pull me out of my doldrums with her playful and irreverent talk, with the persistent display of her naked body beneath sheer cotton fabrics, with her way of not taking me seriously and reproaching me for being gloomy. One day, compelled by desire and loneliness, I put my hand between her thighs. They were slender and welcoming. She changed her position, barely shifting, before pressing her hands on mine and squeezing her legs. We stood up and walked with our arms around each other's waist. We kissed under a tree on the promenade and I felt her buoyant breasts quiver against my chest.

Of all the love affairs I've had, the one that brought Simone and me together was both the most fleeting and the only one I recall without bitterness. That evening, in my studio, we made love with an intensity I could not recall ever feeling before. Simone was all about skin, whether rubbing against a body or against furniture; clothes were like a wrapping in which her body would swim. Her flesh and muscles palpitated, moving in constant defiance and enrichment of the laws of gravity. She didn't know shame. She could sit down to eat, carry on the most incredible conversations, read or write for hours, without covering herself, without showing any modesty or embarrassment. Her body made any place its home.

That was the summer of the parks. I'd pick her up at the cheap hotel where she worked cleaning rooms and making beds and we'd wander around the open spaces of the city. We agreed to save up for a vacation and would economize by buying strawberries, cherries, bread, cheese, and salads, which we'd consume in parks, on terraced steps and in squares. We'd stop and stand in the chalk circles drawn by street artists, we'd listen to the old Revolutionary songs played on a hand organ on one of the bridges of the Île Saint-Louis. Simone knew them all and sang and danced to them, tilting her body, barely moving, receiving the knowing look of the two men singing who knew her since childhood. In the vast Beaubourg plaza I'd insist that we listen to the Andean ensembles or the bands of drums from Senegal and the Congo. We'd sit on the dirty ground littered with cigarette butts, wrappings, and empty bottles to watch the spectacle of the man with the deep hoarse voice who earned a living by putting out live coals with his tongue and spitting out huge flames, or we'd admire the skill of the jugglers, comics, or the youngsters, always different ones, who had come to Paris with a guitar.

Sundays we'd go to an apartment near the Gare de Lyon to have lunch with her father. The place was small and gloomy. Georges would drag one leg and move by straining on aluminum crutches whose bottoms were stained by dirt from the street. With our help he'd prepare traditional stews, bouillabaisses, blood sausage puddings from Auvergne. Her father would always serve a red table wine, which he'd pour for everyone, generously, until the last drop. The dining room was filled with a big cloud of smoke, which couldn't escape through the tiny windows. After dessert, Georges would painstakingly go over to the sideboard, a lit Gitanes dangling between his lips, and bring over a bottle of eau-de-vie. The harsh liqueur hit the stomach, leaving a trail of heat starting from the tongue. Simone and I would end up lying on the couch, gulping down a last glass, smoking one more cigarette, listening to her father starting to snore in his easy chair. Starry eyed, Simone would then leap upon me, in a farce or comedy that was repeated every time and that came close to exhibitionism, ending by shocking me and producing a string of insults that would wrap up the game.

We'd go back to my apartment when the endless twilight would seem to solidify over the still air of the city, when the people around us would be bent on heading home.

One morning I went to visit Sandrine. Since being involved with Simone I had been avoiding her. Marie's senseless accusation had made our attempts to communicate ambiguous and awkward. I knew well the capricious and universal susceptibilities of relationships, especially the ones that could be in the process of becoming exclusive. If I caught her on a bad day, Sandrine could see my new relationship as a betrayal of Marie or even of herself. In these matters, logic and fairness were always precarious. All the same, I valued our friendship and didn't want to lose it. Besides—and perhaps this was what moved me also to visit her—I wanted to know if she had news of Marie.

She had received a letter. She gave it to me to read and I looked for the return address. Marie had written it from the family beach house. She recounted the odyssey of the first days there, the fury that had turned into resignation, exposing the contradictions of her relationship with the mother. She had been admitted to the psychiatric hospital for two weeks and for over a month had been living in her house on the Upper East Side. She liked her psychiatrist, and the medications had helped her, but she still didn't feel well. She would stay home for the summer and then return. Finally, she asked Sandrine to tell me that she would write soon. The letter was filled with news but said nothing important. It felt like she was practicing being sane. Sandrine did not agree. She was happy for her friend and told me it wasn't good (implying that it was very bad) for me to be so suspicious, to see shadows around every corner. Our conversation didn't go much further. I must have caught her on a bad day.

Simone and I were planning our vacation. We were vaguely considering places we'd heard about that appealed to us when one day Simone brought from her father's house an antiquated map of Europe. We spread it out on the bed, spending hours pronouncing the names of all the different places and fabricating impossible itineraries that were more like marathons.

Our modest savings brought us back down to reality. I longed for the sea and for my native tongue; Spain was fairly close, and, in that era before its entry into the Common Market, it was still a cheap country. We decided to trace straight lines and measure them with a ruler. The lines that went to the east coast of Spain were the shortest. Thus we chose our destination. We would try to stretch our money as far as possible so as to be out of Paris for three weeks, in what we hoped would be a cottage by the sea. Every few days we would venture out to the nearest village or city for a change of pace and atmosphere.

Hamed and Sylvie lent us a couple of army rucksacks they had used traveling around North Africa; we filled them with our clothes and a few books, bought our tickets, and finally, sitting face-to-face with our legs entwined, looking out the window of the train, we found ourselves leaving the city. Early the next morning we reached Barcelona, where we planned to stop for a couple of days.

In the Gothic Quarter we chose the hostel whose sign seemed the most weather-beaten, presuming it would cost the least. Once in our own room, we closed the curtains and began to undress standing up. I could feel the amazing heat in Simone's thighs, the soft swell of her belly against my cock. We fell upon the bed causing a creak that made us pause and look at each other in wonder. The furniture was very old, the mattress thin and rutted. Any movement started a symphony of squeaking that must have been audible over the whole floor. Hugging and holding each other close, we fell to the floor. The dirt stuck to the sweat on our bodies. Afterwards, as the morning seeped in like liquid beneath the curtains, we fell into an idyllic sleep.

Later that day we discovered the Ramblas, the Plaça de Catalunya, the towers of the Sagrada Familia, the Sant Jordi church. We walked along the streets near the hostel, taking in the activity of pimps and whores, of dealers in hashish and hard drugs, the Arab and Gypsy enclaves. As the sun set, we made love in the showers of the hostel, wary of any footsteps that drew near, stifling our nervous laughter, moans, and declarations of love.

Later, dining on *gambas al ajillo*, leaning on the bar of a café, among Germans and Scandinavians, barely twenty-four hours after our departure, I felt that Paris was far away. In Barcelona we could breathe new, fresher air. No one knew us; nothing had happened to us on these streets, no history weighed us down.

Everything we needed or wanted was cheap. Espadrilles, packets of unfiltered cigarettes for me, filtered for Simone, a bottle of wine, to which, when the sales clerk told us the price, we quickly added a second. We returned to the hostel late, drunk, and happy to have spent the night discovering the city step by step. All along the dark corridor of the boardinghouse, our hands explored inside each other's clothes, our fingers anticipating, knowing everything.

Once Simone was in bed, dead tired and sleepy, I went to drink from the faucet. The wine, the food, the lovemaking had produced an intense, insatiable thirst. Cupping my hands, I drank at length. The water tasted bad, of salt, of metal. Finally, I fell into the bed that creaked and swayed me like a pendulum.

After two intense and marvelous days, we got up very late. We walked out into a blinding sun. The heat, which in Paris had never had this intensity, was overwhelming. Wandering around the streets, with our clothes soaked, it was so hard to breathe that we were gasping. Nothing tasted right that day, neither the coffee nor the cigarettes nor each other's lips. Simone bared the claws of her bad mood. Realizing we were lost (we didn't have a map and it wasn't easy to find one's way), she directed her fury at me in florid slang. Soon we were fighting, slinging insults that flew out of our mouths like surprises, driving our bodies apart.

We sat back to back under a tree (in a park we never did identify), a big space between us. I turned to watch her smoke, concentrating with a face that made me imagine her childhood tantrums. After the third cigarette smoothed her brow, her eyes met mine and she finally laughed. We made up then and there as we would do many times, in the delicious way lovers do.

We decided to extend our stay in Barcelona for one more day. The city's relaxed contrast with the formality of Paris made us feel like we were on vacation. I insisted upon spending a little time in a museum, though Simone didn't share my enthusiasm. She wandered through the rooms of medieval Catalan art and didn't stay with me when I'd stop in front of paintings, sculptures, and altarpieces. When I'd turn to comment on something, hoping to interest her in the art and ease my worry over her boredom, I wouldn't find her in the gallery. She was two centuries of painting ahead, unmoved by the wonders that surrounded her, sitting barefoot and with her legs crossed on a circular sofa, ready to ask me if we could leave. I was struck by her indifference. She took culture for granted without wanting it or paying it much attention. She was a graduate student in literature, but already I knew her well enough to presume she would not make it to the final dissertation stage. In the future I could see her working in a nursery school or an administrative position or managing a *bouquiniste* stall or a gift shop. What work she did really didn't matter to her. The life she wanted was right in front of her. Unresponsive to the opinions of others on what mattered, she had no ambition. She was satisfied to be the girl who had grown up on the streets of Paris and would always remain on those streets. My artistic aspirations meant nothing to her; Paris had for me a literary aura that said nothing to Simone. She would have preferred me to be simpler, satisfied with a few basic everyday desires, without prospects, spontaneous to the point of oblivion.

That night, the third in Barcelona, I was slow and tired, wanting to return to the hostel to take a bath and read. However, it was hard to curb Simone's energy. We'd stop in front of all the outdoor stands on the Ramblas, we'd watch the street players and wander with the river of people flowing through the streets. The queasiness that would erupt in me the next day was being forged.

We returned to the hostel and I fell asleep almost immediately. There would be no lovemaking gymnastics that night. I had a dream in which Marie appeared. She was sitting on the mattress in my apartment in Paris reading a book with very big pages, and then lifted her eyes and said to me, irritated: "I'm not leaving here."

I awoke at dawn's early light. Simone slept curled up beside me. You could begin to sense the early risers on the street and hear the foghorns in the port. I went to the window and peeked through the curtains. It was a cloudy day, but probably by mid-morning the sun would come out. At eleven thirty we would take the train heading down the coast. We'd buy a ticket as far as Alicante, depending on the landscape we saw out the window: if we saw a place that appealed to us we would get off there and look for a place to stay. It was a risky plan, but we were willing to be adventurous. On the map we had opened in Paris, we saw places with marvelous names: Tabernes de Valldigna, Cabo de la Nao, San Vincente de Paspeig. We imagined an uninhabited peninsula, with a fishing village nearby where we could stock up every few days.

This prospect filled me with enthusiasm. Sun, sea, a primitive lifestyle, giving full reign to our sexuality: all this gave me hope for a personal rebirth and the awakening of a creative period. I saw myself sitting at a rustic table, barefoot, listening to the waves, writing. We wouldn't want for anything more; we were filled with illusions, thinking that we were made for this life and that we now had it within reach.

I felt a vague pain in my abdomen. I dressed and went into the bathroom. I defecated a very liquid diarrhea. I attributed it to the wine, the seafood, and cold cuts. I returned to the room and sat down to read, letting Simone sleep. But before I could even start, I had to return to the toilet several times. I had a headache and felt increasingly unwell.

I had to pull Simone out of her sleep, insisting on the time and rushing her through the process of packing, getting breakfast, and making it to the station. The café au lait and bread and butter, the free breakfast at the guesthouse, didn't agree with me at all. Just a few minutes left before our train was leaving, I had to run to look for the restrooms. I already knew the Turkish toilets, having run into them in Paris, but I was not prepared for the spectacle of that train station toilet. The stink, the collective and overflowing excrement, the polluted puddles that covered the floor and got as far as the door, were overwhelming. My condition did not allow for alternatives and I had to squat, struggling to maintain a perilous balance; falling into that muck would be catastrophic. I sacrificed my handkerchief and dragged my shoes to try to wipe off the dirt.

When I returned to the platform, Simone was shouting from a door. At that moment, the train began to pull away. With my illness and the state of the bathrooms, I had lost track of time. I climbed the steps of the train thinking it would have been better to spend another day in the city.

It was summer and the trains were crowded. My belly produced sounds and I felt waves of pain that didn't allow me to keep still. We ended up finding a place at the end of the car, near the bathroom. There I spent hours sitting on the floor or running in every few seconds, amid bundles and suitcases. I became weaker and sicker and the trip turned into an endless torture. Simone managed to get a cup of hot tea, slices of dry bread, and a couple of antidiarrheal pills, thanks to her enterprising attitude and the solidarity of a couple of Swedes. I hoped to feel better and make it to our incomparable beach.

I was determined and managed to get off at a station whose name I've forgotten. Before arriving, we had seen a rocky coast, with sunny little coves and a deep blue sea that seemed unreal to a Caribbean like myself. It was an effort to carry the rucksack. I had a steady pain in the region of my kidneys.

We walked out of the station and came upon a ghost town. We quickly realized that the area had fallen into the hands of developers who built condominiums that brought little benefit to the town itself, which lay a few kilometers from the coast. The locals remained in the town. The vacationers did not stroll along its streets and basically, upon leaving the station, took taxis to the coast.

On the highway to the beach, leaving town, we decided to hitchhike. I had taken the rucksack off my back and was practically dragging it as we walked along waiting for a ride. The sun was high and there was no shade anywhere.

A pickup truck stopped in front of us. Some bricklayers were going in the direction we wanted. We sat in the back amid tools and bags of cement. The half hour trip did me good. We saw, as we got closer, the blue line of the horizon and the apartment towers that were finished or half-built. We got off in front of a modern-style café and I asked the driver if he knew of some cheap place we could stay, some room or *cabaña*.

"That doesn't exist anymore, man. This place is full of Germans."

He suggested we ask at a bar. In our ignorance, we had arrived at a development composed almost exclusively of apartments for rent, designed to satisfy the needs and expectations of Nordic masses thirsty for sun and fun.

Simone left me with our rucksacks in the outdoor café sipping an herbal tea and went to find out where we could spend the night. She knew neither Spanish nor Catalan, and her English was extremely rudimentary (rather than English it was really only a few dozen words uttered with French syntax and pronunciation). An hour later I saw her returning, furious. She had been in several hotels, which were very expensive and, besides, there were no vacancies. We had been total idiots. This was high tourist season and everything, up to the very last bed, was taken. We would have to return to the town and take the train someplace else or spend the night there as best we could.

Though it might seem surprising, the hope of finding, a few hours later, a comfortable room to spend the night, was erased by the prospect of returning to the torture of the train, and by the uncertainty of where we'd get off and the effort of my having to move again. I suggested that we find a place that wasn't too dangerous and spend the night with one eye opened.

Tomorrow was another day. Simone didn't like the idea, as she already hated that cluster of towers and Nazi tourists, but finally she realized that I wasn't willing to take another step.

The pills had staunched the flow of diarrhea, but I was still weak and sick. We went to the promenade along the sea and later, when night finally fell, with sandwiches and a bottle of water, to one end of the cove. Other couples and some groups of friends were chatting, drinking, and smoking. We decided their company would protect us, and that we could spend the night on the beach there. We calmed ourselves, thinking that this kind of thing happens to everybody sometime.

Soon I fell asleep on the sand. Simone ate and smoked her half-packet ration for the night, putting out the butts, next to one another, on a little mound of sand. The cold woke me a little past two. In the distance, you could see shadows around a bonfire. Near us there was nobody. Simone was resting, sitting up with her sweater on, her hands hidden in her armpits and her legs inside the wool shawl pulled down over her knees. The wind had risen; it was impossible to stay where we were. We moved our things to a wall of rocks at the very end of the half moon. It was damp, but we were more protected. There we waited for dawn, holding each other tightly and rubbing each other's backs, talking and smoking. Sometimes we could hear the laughter of people coming out of the discos and stumbling back to their apartments. At some point we realized that we were happy.

We cursed the Spanish custom of opening late. We had to wait in front of one joint to be able to have coffee, eat, and use the bathroom to shake off the sand we had even in our ears.

On the beach, as the sun was coming up, we had decided to go straight to Alicante. Our adventure had been poorly planned, and we were in no mood to leave anything else to chance. Alicante, a real city, would provide us with a better place to stay for a few days. Besides, it had a beach. There we could find out if some place nearby offered everything we were hoping for.

We arrived by train after midday. We left our rucksacks on the floor of our room in a *pensión* and fell like a ton of bricks onto a bed similar to the one in Barcelona. We woke up at dawn dying of hunger and ate the last package of crackers. As it was too early to do anything else, we must have awakened half the boarding house with our mechanical movements.

In the morning we left with our beach bag to check out the center of town. The city spread out from a hill. It was small and welcoming, with a beautiful seaside promenade. We found out where to take the bus to go to Playa de San Juan. This was a wide stretch of coastline, bordered by outdoor restaurants where you could eat all manner of seafood and paellas. There was practically no vegetation except for palm trees here and there. Beautiful bare mountains rose near the coast. It felt like we were in North Africa more than in Europe. The water wasn't too cold, and the churning sea reminded me of the many afternoons I had spent in my adolescence riding the waves on the beaches of another San Juan.

Simone didn't know how to swim and entered the water, topless, with more determination than bravery. I watched her raise her arms and jump when the waves broke over her. I took her by the hand to where the water covered us and played with her body that gave into me with fear as well as desire. After our swims we'd eat lunch with a big appetite, almost always paella and wine in a little seaside eatery, and take a bus back to the *pensión*, where we'd have a siesta. Later we'd go out for a walk around the city. Night after night we discovered the variety of its bars, the benches in the squares where you could feel the best sea breezes or where at dawn you could drink *horchata* that had the double advantage of quenching one's thirst and tasting delicious. We'd return to the pensíon on deserted streets, holding each other by the waist, stopping to kiss and run our hands over each other, a prelude to the rite of our bodies tanned by the sun, the rite we'd perform all over the hotel room, after which we would sleep. Perhaps there is no other moment of my life in which I remember tastes so clearly. The rice, the wine, the sip of cool water drunk directly from the bottle, the salty taste of Simone's breasts or thighs, these natural delights which gave the impression of being unending, which I felt when she'd whistle a complete and spectacular version of "Le Temps des Cérises" over her glass of beer.

On a side street no more than two meters wide, I discovered a rather well-stocked bookstore. It was the best of the few there were in the city, and it was where readers in Alicante went. Late one afternoon, poking around next to me in the literature section, I met a writer from Valencia. He was a few years older than me and lived a few steps from there, near his administrative job at the Ministry of Education. Instead of living in his city or in Madrid, where he would have liked to work to be in the hub of literary life, he was forced to spend years in provincial institutions before having the seniority necessary to solicit a transfer to the capital. He was teaching in Villajoyosa, which from what he told me had a lot of villa and very little joy. That evening I was alone, as Simone had decided to stay in the *pensión* combining siesta and reading, and having begun a conversation about books and authors with the Valencian, with the usual excess of literary addicts, we ended up moving our exchange to an outdoor café. From there, two hours later, we went to notify our companions, who were impatiently awaiting us, to suggest that we continue the conversation, now with four voices, that very same night at one of the cafeterias along the coastal promenade. Simone and I, drinking a beer while we waited, saw him zigzagging between the tables on the immense terrace, bringing his wife, who also wrote and taught at an institute, and a signed copy of his first book. They spoke very little French, but this fact had not kept them from devouring in the original all of Sartre and Simone de Beauvoir.

Thus began my friendship with Santiago Vergés and Isabel Martínez, and one of the penalties of time and distance has been to lose sight of them. Then, on those long days and nights in Alicante we shared literature, beach, and paella and returned to our dwellings in the wee hours of the morning holding one another in line, kicking our legs like cancan dancers every time we'd hear, coming out of any place, the pounding pasodoble tune of "Paquito el chocolatero."

We were doing so well in Alicante that we had almost forgotten our plan to go off on an adventure. Nevertheless, one Sunday morning, we took an uncomfortable bus to a distant beach to the south of the city, on the way to Murcia. Santiago and Isabel had told us about it. It was sufficiently distant from the tourist centers that the European masses didn't go there and far enough off the beaten track without bars and restaurants that the Spaniards didn't bother to go either in large numbers. Fortified with food and water, we arrived after midday at an arid desertlike coast of stony ledges covered with harsh dry weeds and plants. After walking a while along a path, we reached the top of the dunes. Below stretched an exquisite sea, and a wide expanse of sand dotted with the belongings of a handful of beachcombers. It was hot, and there was no shade anywhere, but there was a cool ocean breeze that felt invigorating.

We decided to take a shortcut, sliding down the slope of the high dune. I was the first to coast on a wave of sand that picked up speed. The mild fear of falling felt like one of life's pleasures, especially for someone like myself, who had spent a whole year without seeing the ocean or feeling its elements. Below, happy and laughing my head off, I recovered the bag of food and shouted to Simone, urging her to come down. But fear made her body stiffen and her fall became a sequence of bumps and somersaults. On the final stretch, her legs flew up in the air and her bikini top rose to her neck. She stopped, all discombobulated, on the verge of crying, her mouth and ears filled with sand. When she heard me laughing, she stood up to chase me.

I let her catch up with me, assuming this would turn into play, but discovered she really wanted to hurt me. Her fists were weak and easy to fend off. In situations like this, it felt like I was dealing with an incomprehensible woman. Finally, more exhausted than anything else, she backed off, took her things, and walked away toward the beach. A few minutes later I caught up with her sitting, smoking, and without the slightest inclination to speak to me. I left her alone and went into the water. If any part of my body came out of the water, it bristled in the wind. I swam further out for the pleasure of the exercise and to warm up. From afar I saw that Simone was lying face up and that one arm covered her eyes. A little later I saw her now on her side, eating what I presumed was an apple. It was impossible to know what was in her head.

During the afternoon the coast became less solitary. Couples, some families, and especially groups of boys populated the wide space of sand with their bags, towels, and beach umbrellas. On a walk by herself, Simone had stopped in front of a man who was using palm leaves to weave hats and birds that looked nothing like the fauna of the Mediterranean. While I had lunch, I watched her stooping in front of him, apparently at ease, speaking very little and listening attentively. The duration of her anger and of this conversation managed to irritate me. The day that was to be a dream had turned into a fiasco from the moment we arrived. I resented the fact that Simone didn't realize this or that she was intentionally prolonging her fury.

I went to where she was talking with the man. I saw her look at me with resignation, as if I were some pesky intruder. She didn't even bother to introduce me. I stood there a while, listening to the conversation filled with banalities. The man spoke French with a Belgian accent.

"Let's go," I said.

"Where?"

"Where our things are."

"Hey, don't you see that I'm busy?"

"Come over for a minute. I have something to tell you."

She stood up with an exaggerated reluctance that awakened my fury. I grabbed her hand and we walked in the direction of our things.

"I'd like to know what you're doing?" she asked, pulling away.

"I want to be with you. We didn't come this far to quarrel."

We got to where we had left our clothes. I came close to her but she didn't respond.

"What's the matter?"

"I am annoyed."

"Why?"

"Because you're a *salaud*."

"You're not being fair. I've done nothing."

"Oh, no? Monsieur never does anything. He never laughs or makes fun of anyone. Monsieur is innocent."

"Come on, Si," I said, naming her by the first syllable, "let it go already."

"I don't feel like it."

"We still have a few hours. Let's have a nice time. Look around you. This is what we wanted to find."

She looked among her things. After several attempts to light it, she bent the tip of a cigarette. I made a cup with my hands and Simone managed to make the cigarette flare up with rapid and deep breaths.

"Thanks," I said ironically.

"*Salaud.*" This time the insult had another tone.

Soon we were in the water. Her breasts glistened in the sun and her nipples were enormous and erect. Simone grabbed onto me when the waves came and I took advantage of her clinging to act out a whole farce of revenge and retributions, which we improvised together, inspired by the joy of our truce. The sun was beginning to cast long shadows, highlighting the rich colors of the sky, sea and earth as its strength gradually faded. The blissful hours had passed too quickly. After a snack, we lay in the sand in each other's arms and gradually our peacefulness turned into sleep.

The wind at sunset roused me suddenly. I sat up and felt surrounded by the almost deserted beach. Alerted by an anxious feeling, I looked for my watch and realized that we were about to miss—if we hadn't already—the bus that would take us back to Alicante. I immediately woke Simone, and we grabbed our things and ran in the direction of the dunes. We climbed up the path as fast as we could. Simone, who smoked like a chimney and never exercised, was flushed and breathless. I ended up thrusting our bag in her hands and running toward the road. Nobody was at the wood shelter that served as a bus stop. Nearby, six people were getting into a Renault 5 and obviously couldn't take us. There was no other car, only a couple of motorcycles and the carcass of a bicycle without wheels, left by someone who knows when. I saw Simone hurrying along the slope where the path in the dunes ended.

"We're fucked," I said.

"What?" she said struggling to catch her breath.

"We got here too late. There's nothing to be done; we missed the bus. Look: there's nobody here."

"What are we going to do?"

"I don't know."

"Hitchhike."

"I guess so, but where? There's no traffic here. We'd have to get to the highway. That's several kilometers away. I hope by the time we get there we still can be seen."

"And these?" She said pointing at the motorcycles. "Maybe they can take us."

"Yes, but where are they, and in any case we can't count on their riders going to Alicante."

"Shit! What a day."

We decided to walk it. The sooner we got to the highway, the more chances we'd have that a driver would stop. I went in front, Simone, two steps behind me. Along the roughly paved road, the dunes gave onto a breakwater piled with boulders. Sometimes we'd feel the fine spray of the salt water that the waves dashed over the rocks.

"How much longer?" I heard her speak after a long silence.

"I don't know. A half hour, an hour; I didn't notice this morning when we came in the bus."

"Nom de Dieu!"

On a curve we saw that someone was walking down the very middle of the road about three hundred meters ahead. It was the Belgian. Simone shouted his name. Some seconds later, the man stopped and looked back. I heard a voice too distant to understand what he was saying, and we saw him put his bag down on the ground and move his arms like a windmill.

This time, when we reached him, I was introduced. Dominique had a hole in his smile. He was missing some teeth.

"We missed the bus," Simone informed him.

He grimaced; I couldn't tell what that meant. A crest of palm leaves stuck out of his bag, above his head. He was carrying, one on top of the other, three hats he had woven and which had not found buyers. Simone, who seemed happy to meet up with someone out in this deserted area, spoke to him in a familiar way that seemed excessive. I participated very little in the conversation, and the thought occurred to me that I might be jealous, but I realized that I really didn't trust the guy.

Dominique said that when we reached the highway, we would most probably find someone to take us to Alicante or, at least, some nearby town where, if we had money, we could hire a taxi. As we had to be seen on the highway, he suggested we cut across the field to get there sooner. We left the road and entered a barely discernible rocky and winding path. Then Dominique asked us to wait, as he had to pee. He took an unusual amount of time and, when I heard him returning from a different direction, I turned around anxiously. I hazily noticed something, and, a second later when he was beside us, I saw the knife. Instinctively, I pushed Simone away, who screamed when she realized we were being attacked. I side-stepped the body that lunged toward me, and moving awkwardly, I managed to hit him in the head with the bag I'd been carrying on my shoulder and which I was now holding onto tightly. Simone, beside herself, was screaming and pleading next to me, moving around the circle we now formed with the Belgian.

"Throw me the bag!"

In it was, aside from our clothes and some leftovers of food, all our money. Giving in meant putting ourselves completely in his hands.

"Come on, give me the bag."

Simone had taken refuge behind me and was trying to reason with him.

"Give me the bag and you can go."

"No, I can't give it to you. Do what you want."

The Belgian was so fast that I realized his attack more by Simone's cry than having seen it. I took one or two steps back and raised my arm to defend myself. I must have slipped, or tripped over a stone, because one of my legs gave way and I fell to the ground. The position of being under him proved my best weapon, because upon trying desperately to stand up, my right leg became entangled with the Belgian's and made him stumble. Then, with the hand that softened my fall, I picked up some dirt and threw it in his face. I grabbed Simone and off we ran. I heard her pleading with words I had never heard her use and I dragged her away shouting, "Run, run!" We stopped, our hearts pounding, behind a grassy hillock. The wind playing with the dry bushes intensified our fear. Behind us one could see the last light of day, a strip of sea and the sliver of a waning moon.

We looked all around us, stuck as if time had frozen. Finally we started running again, trying to get away without really knowing if we were. Our direction kept changing without any order, presuming that this way we were confusing the Belgian, going more or less toward the northeast back to the coast.

We became slightly calmer when we reached the dunes. Further, below, was the beach where we had spent the day. Not a soul could be seen.

The night was long and hard. We were whipped by the wind and the slightest sound put us on the lookout. Our feet, clad only in espadrilles, were hurting, having tripped while running against stones and the roots of plants. For a long time we changed position every fifteen minutes, not because this tactic would prevent in some way a reencounter with the Belgian, but because the wind and the fear prevented us from staying calm. We hid several times and were indecisive about what we should do. We opted, finally, to let the hours pass.

At dawn we were sufficiently calm and rested to continue walking in the direction of the main highway. We were hoping that the Belgian had gone away a while back or that he was sleeping. After a good long walk, Simone glimpsed in the distance the lights of the cars traveling on the highway. Eager to be finished with this nightmare, we walked in single file in that direction.

A couple of hours later we reached the highway to Alicante. Nobody stopped when we tried to hitchhike, probably because they couldn't see us in the dark. With the first light, our hopes increased. Simone could barely remain standing when, in the distance, I caught sight of a taxi. I signaled vigorously and felt like leaping for joy when I saw him stop. The driver lived in a town nearby and was going to Alicante to begin his day's work. During the trip I told him our adventure, and when he left us near the hostel, he refused to charge us. Simone, madly grateful, stuck her head in the window and gave him two noisy kisses.

We entered a café dying of hunger and thirst. We ate and drank in silence, exchanging few words, totally enervated. A little while later, dragging our feet, we made it to our room.

When we got into bed, Simone began to cry. She was crying from a place that only she could know, far beyond us, that room, or Alicante. I consoled her as well as I could, until we both fell asleep.

This experience soured our joy. We did not venture outside of the city again, and even San Juan Beach didn't feel safe. We spent some days as if we were convalescing, afraid to run into the Belgian around any corner. Simone could not be alone, not even in the *pensión*. We walked along the streets as if afraid that something awful might befall us again.

Santiago and Isabel helped us shake off the gloom. We'd meet up with them almost every night and go out to eat tapas in the little restaurants along the coast. Thanks to Santiago, some months later, I would see my first stories published in a Madrid magazine and, afterwards, I would become its stringer in Paris, sending movie reviews and critiques of the latest literary works.

The incident on the beach changed the way I felt about Simone. I now allowed myself to identify traits and attitudes in her that I had never liked but had ignored, perhaps motivated by my hopes for novelty or a fresh start. Her frequent and perplexing mood changes, the extremes of certain emotions unleashed by seemingly minor incidents, her lack of prudence disguised presumably as spontaneity, just like her disappointing and sometimes embarrassing indifference to culture: all these were aspects which, I realized, had always affected me whether or not I'd wanted to admit it. On the other hand, however, there was her joyful manner and our rich sexuality. One fact, whether or not it was fair, was crucial to my malaise: I blamed her for the incident with the Belgian. We hadn't talked about it, but at certain moments in that endless night and in the days that followed, I caught her brooding over her foolishness. The look in my eyes must have betrayed me, because more than once she asked what I was thinking. I always hesitated to answer and would look away, pretending that I was distracted. "Nothing," I'd say, and ask her about anything that would change the subject.

We'd been together barely three or four months, but the intensity of what we had lived, our almost exclusive concentration on each other, the trip to Spain, and the way in which I had forgotten Marie over that period, allowed us to feel as if we had been together much longer. We didn't realize that the relationship was already in decline.

We wanted to stay in Alicante one more week but were very low on money. Too many unforeseen expenses, books and cassettes, too many tapas and bottles of wine, were boring a hole in our pockets. We could only extend our stay for four more days. Enough to take our last walks and swims at San Juan Beach, and for the final dinners with Santiago and Isabel, who, conscious of our lack of funds, treated us on several occasions.

Around nine o'clock on a late-summer evening we boarded the express train that would follow the coast, passing Valencia and Barcelona before reaching the border at Irun. We passively watched the scenery go by with the low spirits of a trip's end, without any desire to talk much. In Paris the exams I hadn't taken in June awaited me. Their subject matter seemed lost in time and merely thinking about them was enough to depress me.

After a night of interrupted sleep, we got off at Austerlitz station and parted on the metro platforms. Simone was going to visit her father, to get clean clothes, to ask if she could find work again at the hotel, and the next day, she would go back to my place. I went to my studio on the Impasse de l'Astrolabe. Paris looked like an old postcard: a familiar panorama that I observed with strange indifference. As I entered my building, I opened the mailbox. It was filled with junk mail, but there was also a fistful of letters. I examined the envelopes stamped in San Juan or New York, the one from my parents containing a much-needed check, and I counted three letters of different thickness with my address in Marie's tiny handwriting.

I organized them to read them in the order they had been sent. The first went on for five pages in lines that scrawled downward. Knowing her, I knew they had been written in bed. She recounted, grosso modo, the heartbreaking tale of her disappearance. Her mother had hired a lawyer to have her declared incapacitated and thus to place her under the guardianship of the family. An ambulance had taken her to the airport and on that same day—it was nighttime in New York—she was admitted to a psychiatric hospital. There she discovered the consequences of her act. Her ward companions terrified her. She was in a world of madmen and she realized she had crossed a line. This more than anything else forced her to react. She didn't want to be one of those incurable crazies who have conversations with themselves and repeat absurd gestures. That first night, she became determined to get out of there as soon as possible. She managed to get Dr. Simmons to discharge her and to administer the rest of her treatment at her parents' home.

The last two pages were about us. They included a complicated reflection on what Marie called "our time" without clarifying whether she meant past, present, or future. She asked me to write to her, to forgive her, not to forget her. I folded the pages and put them back in the envelope thinking of them as a message in a bottle that had drifted to shore from a shipwreck in a distant ocean. I realized how much Simone and Spain had made me forget. I didn't want to brood over the sordid aspects of the letter and preferred to ignore what it implied about me.

The second letter had been written twenty days later. It was very short, and barely covered one side of a small sheet. It began by reminding me that she had written to me and had not received an answer. She presumed cynically that the absence of news implied that I was having a blast. She couldn't believe that our entire past deserved nothing more than this disregard. The letter stopped at the end of this paragraph, without any farewell salutation. Below, without anything further, was her signature.

A familiar unhappiness took hold of me. Once again I witnessed the zigzag of her emotions, without being able to interrupt—or to respond. The city, which so recently had been stripped of its old associations, once again rolled over me with the patina of all that I had endured. Her depressive complaints, more than the pain of loss and nostalgia, brought Marie back into my life.

The third envelope contained something thick. I felt it, putting off opening it for a moment. In it there was only a cassette. I went over to the radio and put it in the player, but before pressing the "play" button, I paused: the idea that I was going to hear Marie's voice again made me stop dead. I resisted for just a minute, knowing that I would give in.

I realized I was, in some way, betraying Simone, but I sat

down at the desk with a cigarette and coffee. Marie spoke as she had so many times before, from the hallowed place that had room for only the two of us. In her monologue I heard pauses and transitions that seemed to contain my responses, the phantom of our dialogue. Now nothing remained of the edginess of her second letter or the clinical case history of the first. As I listened I became aware of the powerful bond between us, which despite everything endured.

Marie signed off, but I stayed at the desk until the tape stopped automatically. I felt a joy words could not describe, a joy unlike the passion inspired by Simone. My feelings for Marie touched other places in my past and my being, like a palimpsest of our life, something I couldn't destroy without destroying myself.

Even while knowing it would upset me, I wrote to Marie that very evening. I spoke of what her voice had awakened in me. To explain my silence, I told her I had just spent a few weeks in Spain. I didn't mention Simone or go into any details. Thus I committed a vile act toward both of them, but at that moment I could do nothing else.

4

I had missed the June session exam on indigenous literature.
I used those afternoons to refamiliarize myself with my notes
and readings. I buried myself in new books and the image of
Klok returned to accompany me day and night.

Simone was also studying for an exam, in her case French
literature, and was reading (in bed) an awe-inspiring succes-
sion of hefty tomes. After those weeks in Spain, our life together started to feel boring, punctuated by dormant inter-
vals. Even the sex lost its vitality. We started to feel like an old
married couple, stuck at home. The exciting times of mutual
discovery lay behind us.

My interest in the aboriginal world lasted well past the day
of the exam. I'd go to bookstores, especially the FNAC and
L'Harmattan, in search of old French and Spanish chronicles
and contemporary ethnology books. I read all the essays of
Pierre Plon, including his marvelous translations of myths and
song cycles.

One day, when Simone was busy with chores, I went to the
Musée de l'Homme and spent the whole morning and part of
the afternoon wandering in its rooms. I would stop to draw
and to take notes in front of display windows, which had
never been changed (as I knew from having seen photos of
the era) since Picasso had discovered African art and Iberian
sculptures there during that extraordinary moment of cross-
fertilization that gave birth to cubism and so many other artistic revolutions.

I walked out dazzled and famished and went straight to a
café near the Trocadéro palace to have lunch and prolong my

state of enchantment. I sat down at a table and took a book by Pierre Plon out of my shoulder bag. I ordered food and started reading. A little later, biting into my Gruyère sandwich, I couldn't help noticing my neighbors at the next table. A heavy-set older Frenchman was sitting next to a thin, very small woman with Asian features. They were chatting with a stout woman with dyed blonde hair, and I soon gathered that the couple was married and the bleached blonde, who was the man's sister, had just met her sister-in-law. The blonde spoke of racism among the French with an extraordinary lack of tact. It was obvious the siblings hadn't seen each other for some time. From the way she dressed and acted, spouting clichés and a nationalistic, xenophobic view of France—more common than one expected in spite of the city's much-touted cosmopolitanism—the blonde woman seemed to be from humble origins. Their conversation quickly degenerated into an argument and reached an impasse, making them all uncomfortable. But then the man spoke with extraordinary calm, deflecting any stormy confrontation. His wife, who was Vietnamese, and who, by her age, I imagined had lived through the war, also mediated in her somewhat limited French, and with a cool head dodged the low blows of her sister-in-law. It was truly fascinating to watch them from behind the screen of my book.

The sister stood up to say good-bye, halfheartedly inviting them to dinner. I figured they wouldn't be seeing each other again for a long time.

"What do you make of that?" asked the man when his sister had left.

"Hatred leaves scars on those who cultivate it," said his wife.

"Yes, no doubt. I can assure you hers is a sterile existence, and what's worse, she doesn't even realize it because she sees herself as white and French and therefore superior, compared to your people."

"How tragic."

"What can we do? There are so many like that."

"I know. In Saigon they were worse."

Out of her cloth bag, the woman took a very long pipe, as long as her forearm; on its end was a small, carved bowl for the tobacco. It was not only strange to see a woman smoking a pipe, but also the style of her pipe was very striking. The man asked for two more coffees (I took advantage of the waiter's proximity to order mine), and he took out of his jacket pocket another pipe, this one of an ordinary size.

During the conversation with his sister, the man had glanced in the direction of my table several times. I didn't know what could be catching his attention, as he seemed to focus either on the ashtray or on my hands. I was intrigued. I took out a cigarette and discovered I didn't have anything to light it with. I asked my neighbors for a light.

"Tenez," said the man, and placed a box of matches on my table.

"Merci bien, monsieur," I answered.

"Regarde, il lit le bouquin de Pierre," said the woman who looked over and smiled.

Suddenly it was clear: the man had been looking at the book in my hands. My passion for this text, and perhaps also my visit to the museum, emboldened me.

"Do you folks know Pierre Plon?"

"Yes, we know him. He was our friend. "D'ou venez-vous, monsieur?" asked the man, who must have noticed my accent.

"De Porto Rico."

"Ah, bon!" the woman sounded surprised.

Following the protocol of formality with which strangers address each other in France, we started talking. Plon provided a bond between us, for my keen interest in him and his work visibly pleased my interlocutors. I learned from the Frenchman that the ethnologist had been his friend ever since the two of them had first entered the classrooms of the Sorbonne, almost three decades earlier. Plon had then embarked on his scholarly vocation and had become, according to this man, not only a great field research scientist and an astute theoretician but also the poet who introduced to French scholars and academics the spoken word of the indigenous peoples. Plon knew what those words meant, since, in his unfinished work, he not only wrote papers for specialists but also had reconstructed the imaginary world of the Indians, allowing anyone with curiosity and intelligence to gain entry to a culture that revealed to us how much we had lost.

I told them I had just spent hours in the Musée de l'Homme taking notes and sketching in front of the Amazon display windows.

"That collection is quite outdated and incomplete, but I admit that it is fascinating. I understand your interest. May I take a look at your notebook?"

I put it on his table. The man leafed through the pages, identifying objects and tribes from my crude and sometimes schematic sketches, and asking me if I knew certain texts and catalogs, commenting that in Berlin, Hamburg, Brussels, and Stockholm there were feather necklaces and domestic objects that outdid the beauty and ethnological fascination of those to be found in Paris.

I told them I was sorry about the death of Plon, that I would have loved to have known him, and that, being a literature student, the encounter with his work had made me contemplate the possibility of changing my research plans and university center in order to study the primitive world.

"The day he died in the traffic accident, that very same day," said the man, "he was supposed to come to our house for dinner. Believe me, sir, you cannot imagine what his loss has meant to me."

The woman was slowly smoking her long pipe. "Perhaps

you might like to come to our house to see photographs of
Pierre's expeditions," she said, the words curling out of her
mouth at the same pace as the smoke.

"I would love to."

The man gave me their names and address, and the date and
time of the appointment. I hesitated as I wrote his last name
in my notebook and asked him to repeat it.

"Don't worry, sir. It's easier than you think. Look in the first
page of the book you have on your table. There you will see it
written. So then, see you in a few days. It has been a pleasure
to meet a young reader of Pierre's."

We shook hands smiling and I watched them leave the café.
The man tenderly put his big hand on the skeletal nape of the
woman's neck. As soon as I lost sight of them, I opened the
book. On the page that followed the title page there were
only three words: "To Didier Pétrement." Plon had dedicated
to him his translation.

I was in the vicinity of the Pétrements' building before the appointed time. Normally I was punctual and when I would first
visit someone new, I would make sure to leave enough time.
On this occasion my expectations created by our first meeting made me arrive a half hour early. Etiquette did not allow
for ringing the bell before I was expected, so I killed time going to a café around the block. They lived on the southeastern
edge of the city, near the *autopiste périphérique*. The museum of
Asian antiquities was not far off.

My enthusiasm about this visit had made Simone uncomfortable. She didn't like the intelligentsia, that large sector of
people who thought, wrote, and created, and who in France,
unlike other countries, were not dedicated exclusively to
teaching or to administration. More than anything else, her
antipathies revealed her natural tendencies, her desire to

complicate her existence as little as possible and to live in the stability of Paris, which had always been her home, with an inertia that was the enemy of questioning and change.

At the appointed hour I went up to the third floor. The smiling corpulence of Didier Pétrement appeared in the doorway. On all the shelves in the apartment there were books and papers, as well as large clay pottery without the glossy finish of enamel or the usual polish of Chinese or Japanese porcelain, which, judging by their rustic look and tarnished coloring, must have belonged to more ancient cultures. We went to sit around their work desk. Behind Pétrement was a canvas painted in dark ochers and reds with scenes from the life of the Buddha. Sometime later I would learn that the unframed silk wall hanging was a Tibetan tanka created in Dharamsala by artists in the Dalai Lama's circle. On the table were piles of thick books. Some of those lying opened contained illustrations of works of art and texts written in Oriental alphabets. I was expecting to enter a world like the one the character of Neptune encounters when he follows Klok, but here I did not see any object from the Amazon or anything remotely American. Pétrement must have noticed my surprise because he took the initiative to explain.

"As you can see, Pierre and I took different paths. He went toward America, and I toward Asia. I studied at the School of Eastern Languages and specialized in the Far East, especially the Khmer and Vietnamese cultures, even though I originally studied Chinese and Sanskrit."

"I see."

"Don't feel cheated. The Tupi-Guarani peoples resemble the ethnicities of the Golden Triangle more than one might assume, and I followed Pierre's research for something more than friendship. Later, Son will show you the photographs we promised you. But let me offer you coffee, and do tell me who you are, and why you're here in Paris."

In over a year no French person had asked me this question. Such courtesy was considered unnecessary because the city was one of the centers of the world, and my wanting to be there, like any foreigner, was taken for granted. We were attracted to French culture and its natives did little to inquire about our circumstances.

I began giving Pétrement some basic information. I spoke of my studies, of my desire to write, of the interests that had led me to become enthusiastic about Plon; but the warmth of his listening encouraged me to enter into personal details. I spoke of my hard times, of Marie's suicide attempt, of the loneliness I had experienced in the city and how reading Neptune and the world Plon had opened to me had made it possible, in so many ways, for me to keep going.

Pétrement listened to me, smoking one of the pipes he had lined up on his desk, sipping the coffee that Son, his wife, had brought with a smile and a slight bow, before sitting down to participate in the conversation and also to light up her long pipe.

When I had finished, Pétrement responded: "I see that at your age you have lived a lot and suffered quite a bit. It must not have been easy for you to remain in this city, which in so many ways is not welcoming. It's true that here there are, as everywhere, good people. But I must add that they are also well hidden."

"I met a Puerto Rican in Saigon," said Son. "He was with the Americans, fighting."

"He was forced to," I said.

"I know; that's why war is tragic."

"I don't know if you know," said Pétrement, "that Pierre did not get to teach in the university until shortly before he died. For the academy, the cultures of the Amazon were almost totally lacking in interest. They didn't have the prestige of the great pre-Columbian civilizations. Many still share the view-

point of the conquistadores, except that now they're looking
for the gold of the dead. The Indians who interested Pierre
were nomads; they didn't build anything lasting and walked
around naked. Lévi-Strauss opened a theoretical path, but
Pierre's writings were groundbreaking, that is, his complex
and human portrait of those beings on the verge of extermi-
nation. Our spiritual poverty, I mean the typical Westerner's,
even among the well educated, is a bottomless pit."

After striking a match and lighting his pipe again, he added:
"To a certain extent I was prey to those prejudices. I began
studying Chinese and Sanskrit, the Buddhist and Taoist cultures, and all this was worthwhile. It has greatly enriched me.
However, one day I obtained a position at the Alliance Française and they sent me to Phnom Penh in Kampuchea. Over
the years I traveled in Laos, Thailand, Burma, and Vietnam.
Aside from the national languages, I learned the languages of
the mountain villages, and after leaving the Alliance, I spent
long periods of time with some of them. I didn't have the
confidence to make myself the voice of Pierre's memory and
carry out his legacy. Besides, many of those peoples are still
living, though they grow more and more bitter and alien-
ated by modernity. Anyway, in France and in other parts of
Europe, we lack the obsessive passion for archeology. If a culture works in stone or metals, we can dig up its knickknacks
and put them in a museum. What hasn't been noted is that
those institutions are gigantic mausoleums. There is nothing
living there. The story of Neptune you refer to is divine but
tragically describes an impossible wish."

I would soon find out that Pétrement earned his living taking care of and cataloging those knickknacks whose concep-
tual status he condemned. He worked with temporary con-
tracts in museums, feeling perpetually exploited by those he
called "catalog scribes."

Son brought in an envelope that contained twenty odd

photos. Plon appeared on beaches, in restaurants, on moun-
taintops, and in the jungle surrounded by children of all ages
or perched on the branch of a tree, making notes in a notebook. One of the photos showed the ethnologist and Pétrement, their arms around each other's shoulders, smiling at
the camera. They seemed very young. Didier took it from the
table and looked at it a long while. Then he stood up and went
to find something in a wardrobe. He returned with a notebook with stains on the cover. Those patches of dampness and
mold looked tropical, like those growing on my old books
and drawings left in San Juan.

"Before you leave, I'd like to show you . . ." he said while
he opened it. "Here Pierre wrote a draft of the myths and leg-
ends. Take a look: from this side, on the pages on the left, is
the original, recorded phonetically, and on the right, you can
see the first French version. I don't know if you know that he
wasn't the first to undertake this task."

"Helvio Piglia."

"I see that your interest is serious. Few people know that
Paraguayan priest who ruined his reputation by dedicating
himself to the Indians. Unfortunately, I don't know Spanish,
but at some point Pierre showed me those very poor editions,
printed in Asunción at the clergy's expense, in which some
of the myths and stories of the hunters came out for the first
time. Pierre got to meet him and was very impressed. I am convinced that one of the merits of my friend's work was to give
continuity to those efforts of Piglia's which otherwise would
have remained in the darkest obscurity. Life moves in mysterious ways. Can you imagine Piglia thinking that one day his
books would reach the hands of an anthropology student in
Paris and that the latter would decide to abandon the usual
routes of his profession and end up taking a plane to go and
meet the man who had gathered the Word from a people lost
in the Chaco jungle?"

Pétrement spoke with the gestures and portentous intona-
tion of the educated French, who, even before the Enlight-
enment, had inherited the enjoyment of words and an intellectual tradition. It was fascinating. I felt honored by the
Orientalist's generosity but at the same time realized that his
devotion to knowledge, in particular a specialized knowledge
that belonged to a minority, would find in French culture and
society the kind of support that made it intelligible and even
prestigious. In my country such an attitude was impossible.
This scholarly outlook might be sustainable in certain great
cities, in which curiosity could lead one to exercise any geographical, cultural, linguistic, or historical vocation. In my
world, cultural space was too small and fragile, and the idea
of pursuing poetry, dance, art, or anything not connected to
business and dreams of financial fortune, seemed laughable.

Our conversation had lasted a couple of hours, and the moment to take my leave was approaching. I didn't want this to
be our only encounter, but I had nothing to offer Pétrement.

"Dear friend, I must return to the pains of my labor. Monsieur Dors wants, without delay, to sign off on a research
project that will establish the mediocrity with which the foun-
dational text of Pantanjali has been approached, and he is being so beastly that I have no relief. Let me assure you that we
have enjoyed your visit and we would love to see you again."

"Perhaps our friend," Son interrupted, "would like to come
join us at Monsieur Nan's lecture?"

"He's a Buddhist monk from Vietnam," explained Pétrement. "He has lived in France since the war: an admirable man,
a man engaged in contemporary culture besides being a great
master and poet. Next week he will give a talk in Paris. We
would love you to join us."

"Thank you so much. Do give me the information and I'll be
sure to be there."

Before we said good-bye, Son gave me a piece of paper in

which she had noted down—with the difficulty of one who, rather than write, draws each letter—the name of the lecture hall, the street, and number.

I walked a while before returning to Impasse de l'Astrolabe. What I had just experienced as a Caribbean with my interests and background was a dream: talking about the Vedas, the Chan tradition, or the mythology of the Amazon tribes with all naturalness, as if these were everyday matters. Here, while I was in Paris, such flirtations with a scholarly vocation seemed possible. One day, however, I would return to San Juan. It was one thing to be interested in Neptune, who doubtlessly some people there might have heard of, and a very different thing to study cultures or areas of knowledge that were unknown or nonexistent to most of my countrymen. I had suffered a great deal because of my difference, but that didn't matter then. I was far away and could allow myself everything, even what I had always yearned for.

Immersed in these thoughts, I arrived home. Simone was listening to a detestable cassette at top volume: a selection from early rock, teenage dance music which, in France, anachronistically, still created a furor. I turned the volume down and lay in bed. I had no desire to tell her about my afternoon, and pretending to be exhausted, I tried to hide the fact that Simone's presence, at such moments, was as unpleasant as the music.

Almost without noticing, we began to spend less time together. One day she went to see her father and told me she would spend the weekend with him and I did nothing to stop her; on another occasion I came up with an excuse so as not to go to a party with her, and after that the excuses weren't difficult.

Sometimes we'd go to bed and make love with a heartbreaking intensity. We'd look at each other, conscious of what was happening, but wouldn't say a word. I didn't want to lose her, but I couldn't change her. And this was new, because despite what I would have been willing to admit to myself, I had tried to change Marie. But with Simone, from the start I knew I was defeated. All my persuasiveness would never make her budge.

The Pétrements contributed, without any intention on their part, to the decline of our relationship. Their world, in which Simone hadn't the remotest interest, was too persistently appealing to me. And on the other hand, letters and cassettes kept arriving from New York. I'd answer them on the sly, informing Marie of my new acquaintances and of the direction my interests were taking. I didn't share my intellectual life with Simone, nor had I found any other woman I could connect with in that way.

One day the inevitable happened. I left a cassette from Marie on the recorder and Simone, who wanted to listen to music and was alone in the studio, heard it from beginning to end. She didn't know Spanish but it wasn't difficult to interpret the intonations, the playful tenderness, or to understand the conjugations of the verbs for *love*. When I arrived, I found her waiting in bed.

"What's this?" she asked with the cassette in her hand.

Despite the impact of the surprise, which at first left me speechless, awkwardly trying to come up with reasons, I tried to be honest. But it was too late, as I had hidden from her the very existence of the letters. I said nothing, avoiding her eyes. This was easier, and perhaps also better. Simone got out of bed and went to get her bag.

"I'm leaving. Don't come near me. I don't want to see you."

In spite of her words, she seemed calm.

"Don't come looking for me at my father's house. Keep dreaming of your *nana*. Keep making your love tapes for her."

Near the door we bumped into each other head on. I went to hug her and received a push followed by a rain of blows mixed with moans. Simone must have had in her bag, which she used almost like a whip, some of her Stendhal and Balzac novels, probably in the Classiques Garnier critical editions, because a few of her blows left my skull vibrating. I finally managed to grab her and, with difficulty, while she kicked and cursed her head off, I picked her straight up until the two of us fell onto the bed. The struggling continued a bit more, and when I finally became concerned that she was seriously fighting me, I saw she was smiling and crying all at once. All I could do was smile, too, at which point I received a punch, the only real blow in the whole scene.

"Don't you dare smile, because then I really won't forgive you!"

We were both motivated by love, which despite it all, understands.

We ended up stripping each other naked and staying in bed until nightfall. I told her what I knew of Marie. She listened to me in silence, sometimes playing with my hair, smoking one cigarette after another. I never knew what she really thought, but there's no doubt that when I recall my love affairs, the fact that Simone didn't leave that evening was a high point, poignant and vivid.

They called him Monsieur Nan or Le Petit Vietnamien, and the patronizing touch contained tenderness much more than contempt. He was a sixty-year-old man who looked surprisingly young. Dozens of enthusiasts had come to listen to him in a union hall. Later I would learn that the choice of venue wasn't accidental. Monsieur Nan, despite the ethereal aura he produced, had been an indefatigable social worker. He had protested at the United Nations and the European Parliament, organized and participated in expeditions to save the boat people, written dozens of books, and founded a monastic community in Switzerland in which there were equal numbers of men and women from West and East.

I had never heard of him before and watched his attendants in their long dark robes, and the audience, which seemed like a pretty eccentric gathering, with unease. Nan appeared on the platform, greeting the audience with his hands together. The spectators did not applaud; many of them, including the Pétrements, stood up and returned his greeting with their hands joined and a bow of the head. The Vietnamese man went to sit on a low podium covered by a rug, upon which there was a meditation cushion. Beside him were a large metal bowl and a wooden mallet with which Nan rubbed the edge, creating a sound that filled the room with a lingering vibration.

"Let us be conscious of our breathing," he spoke with a thick accent. "If our breaths are short and nervous, we feel this short and nervous breathing. If it is long and peaceful, we also feel it enter, course through our body, and leave."

The hall remained silent. Nan had collected himself without transition, feeling the breath pass through his body. Pétrement had warned me. He invited me not to be prejudiced by the technique's apparent simplicity. Behind its modest façade one would find knowledge acquired over the millennia. The Buddha had done nothing but breathe, and had understood. Thus he liberated himself, on a memorable night, beneath the shelter of a tree, by conquering the hordes of Maya, hence dispelling the mirror of illusion.

After a few minutes, Nan rubbed the vessel again, and when the sound faded out in the hall, he began his talk. His discussion was not esoteric claptrap. Without any drama, without shouldering the suffering of the world, he spoke with amazing lucidity, illustrating the connection between emotion, word, and action with the following: the rain, an exploited third-world peasant, and the plate of food on a French table that one took for granted. He saw the relationship between war and inner confusion, between unconsciousness and error. He questioned the coordinates of personal identity upon which almost all of Western civilization had been erected. He asked who suffers when we suffer. Do we suffer? Or is suffering the set of circumstances and inner space we create for it?

My ignorance was total. I had only vague ideas about the East. Hinduism, Buddhism, Taoism were, at that time, an undifferentiated whole for me, doubtlessly worthy of appreciation and respect, but very remote. I was, however, struck by Didier Pétrement's reverence for this man. In Son one could assume devotion to her own culture, but the Orientalist had demonstrated a dedication I couldn't dismiss.

The evening ended with a longer meditation followed by a Q&A in which Nan was brilliant. The Pétrements invited me to come with them to greet him, as they also wanted to introduce me. Totally embarrassed by how he bowed to me smiling, I watched him take my hands in his. At the hall entrance, his collaborators were selling his books and I bought one. In this way I began to develop an enthusiasm equal to my involvement with indigenous cultures and literature.

A few days later I found in my mailbox a package from Marie. After the argument with Simone, and with her full knowledge, I had sent Marie Neptune's novel and copies of some of my texts. For most of my life abroad, Marie had been my first and sometimes my only reader. I valued her opinions and criticism, especially since none of my French friends could read in Spanish. Simone didn't object, accepting, at least for now anyway, that between Marie and myself there was a bond she couldn't surpass.

Marie wrote to me after having devoured *Rue de Babylone*. The range of characters and stories in Neptune's world had given her a whiff of another atmosphere and an opportunity to lay aside her preoccupations. And she had read my texts and responded with disproportionate enthusiasm, which was probably a form of gratitude and seduction rather than critical appraisal. However, a young writer's thirst for approval didn't allow me to notice such subtleties, and I took pleasure in reading her letter several times, as if Marie's response could be that of all possible and imaginable readers. The package also contained a hardcover notebook of very fine paper and a small box with a fountain pen. On it she had written a note: "So that you will write and write and write."

The gifts meant so much to me. Not only did I enjoy these objects in themselves, but also the pleasure of seeing Marie reach out to me, which I experienced from the perspective of nostalgia. Despite my efforts and the struggles of our lives, I couldn't (and perhaps didn't want to) break free from her. I didn't realize the extent to which my love was a ball and chain—in a way, an illness I couldn't shake—a dependency, in brief, a stupidity. I still couldn't forget the sweetness we had so often shared.

During those days I used the notebook for the first time. I began a novel I would work on for the next two or three years and that would accompany me when I returned to my country. I wanted to tell the story in these pages. A writer always returns to the same sources, even if afterwards the texts he presents to the public erase the traces. At that time, I was writing from inside the story, without knowing the outcome, struggling to find a meaning, a tone, and a denouement. The book wasn't totally bad, and an editor was on the verge of publishing it, but I am grateful for his hesitation, which allowed me to return, again and again, to that time in Paris, fighting with memory, giving into the pain.

When I had already finished my exams and it was almost time for the new academic year to begin, I received in the morning mail a note from Pétrement inviting me to come by his house. He had just signed a contract that called for a great deal of work, most of it tedious, consisting, among other things, of producing notes on hundreds of file cards, and he was proposing to make me his assistant. I accepted immediately. More than the money, which would come in handy, the opportunity of working at his side appealed to me, spending hours in the smoky gloom of their apartment, watching Son come and go without a single floorboard creaking under her weight. That year, all I had to do was attend a dissertation seminar. The rest of my time I could use to read, write, and work.

My task was to catalog the collections of Tibetan sculpture and objects in several French and foreign institutions in order to present them to the commissioners of an exhibit with encyclopedic pretensions, which would be inaugurated in the Grand Palais and travel afterwards to other countries. Pétrement would be in charge of the research, as well as dealing with the museums and shaping the collection. My work consisted of producing a clean copy of the findings and organizing the data (size, date, place of origin, etc.) in a preestablished format.

I began going two afternoons a week but soon they extended the job to three, with frequent invitations to dinner. I would work diligently, but the Pétrements loved to chat, pause for tea or coffee and a smoke on their pipes, or—why not?—two or three. Son bombarded me with her questions about Simone and Marie, Puerto Rican cuisine, or the history of my ancestors. At my slightest query, often barely formulated, Didier would jump at the chance to vanish into his library and bring down, from the upper shelves, books by German Sinologists, or parallel versions (Sanskrit, Pali, and Chinese with their corresponding translations into English or German) of the Buddha's long and midlength speeches. This was such a complex and fascinating world that, on the occasions that I went by the university, discussions of certain lengthy nineteenth-century French or English novels left me cold and wondering how could I waste time like that.

On the face of it, Simone had adapted to the new order. We were living together, tolerating each other's absences, which grew longer and longer. Sometimes I'd return to the studio to find a note informing me that she was staying at her father's house or was going out to eat with Sylvie and Hamed. We entertained and kept each other company, but the spring was drying up.

One night, returning home from a leisurely dinner and conversation with the Pétrements, I found her waiting for me. I saw her suitcase in the kitchen and I imagined the worst.

"I'm not breaking up with you, but it would be better if we didn't live together for a while. It's no longer the same and we need a change."

"What do you mean?"

"You know what I mean."

"Yes, I know, but what's left?"

"Don't make a scene. No reason to see it that way. I want to be far away for a few days. Then we'll see. By the way," she added, "I don't have anyone else."

"Neither do I."

"Well, you have Marie."

"Don't be silly. She's on another continent."

"But you still have her."

"That's not true."

"Let's not talk about it now. It's better this way. I'm not complaining, but neither am I fooling myself about your *nana* and this doesn't take anything away from what we've experienced together. I don't even know if she has anything to do with my desire to leave. It's not only you, or her. In the end, this always happens. I don't want us to end badly. This is simply the way I am, and whatever happens I know I won't forget you."

The conversation had rapidly led us over a line, had become a good-bye.

"Stay a few more days," I said, feeling my heart in my throat. "Maybe we can be like before, go someplace together."

"That's not it, and besides, I have no money."

I went to sit next to her on the bed and we embraced. I tried to pull her closer, to keep her from getting up.

"No. I'm going to miss the last metro."

5

98 A period began in which I was often grateful for having sat at that table in a café next to the Musée de l'Homme. The Pétrements were my only friends. I saw Simone a few times in cafés and squares, but she would not return to my studio, not even to retrieve her last belongings. Sandrine, meanwhile, resented my distance and paid in kind. I spent weekends between the radio and my books, going out for a walk when the walls started to close in on me. Paris became a desert once again.

The new order of things was apparent even in my relations with Didier and Son. The file cards were boring and often I just didn't feel like listening to the Orientalist rant about a broad gamut of French institutions. At the same time, I became tired of witnessing the couple's arguments; they now felt comfortable enough in my presence not to hide their rough edges.

As the afternoons grew shorter I would head for the metro, where I'd see the exhausted faces of the passengers, with big dark bags under their eyes. In spite of its cachet, Paris was like any other place. Solitude was doled out everywhere and life did not offer consolations. Happiness seemed far away. I had no one despite the thousands of faces, the millions of hands.

I'd settle at a corner table in Au Chien Qui Fume. I'd always bring books, notebooks, and pens, but soon I would leave them behind and simply spend an hour smoking and looking around as I slowly sipped one or two espressos. I'd manage to feel something close to contentment. The constant activity on the street and watching the passersby had a pacifying effect. My mind wandered from one idea to another until I lost track of words altogether and found myself, for minutes at a time, essentially unconscious. These were the best moments, but all the same they left me feeling lost.

I began to paint again and would kill time sketching faces on pieces of cardboard that I'd bring in from the street. The walls of my studio became covered with eyes, looking at me, from numerous variations on the same head I persisted in drawing time and again. All sorts of marginal types—from actors who improvised their performances on the street to nocturnal loners at the bars in cafes—inhabited my fantasies and became, as it were, my traveling companions. I chronicled their fates without missing a detail, to justify my own.

When I'd been living this life for three months, I received a letter from Marie announcing her return. She begged me to go and get the key to her apartment at her aunt's house, because she didn't want to have to see her when she arrived. She also asked me to come pick her up at the airport. She would soon let me know the date we would see each other again.

This news became my salvation. I had the impression that something fundamental was changing. Marie and I would usually reinforce each other's weaknesses, which, more than love or mutual understanding, had sealed our bond. From the moment I received her letter I did nothing but wait. The days and weeks became endless, and I was influenced obsessively by expectations along with hopes I couldn't shake and which—against all common sense—I went on building around her arrival.

I cleaned her apartment as well as my own; I bought flowers that withered and which I had to keep replacing. I didn't show up for the thesis seminar or for work, as if in this way I could make Marie arrive sooner. Finally, late one afternoon, after having checked my mailbox compulsively, I received a telegram. Marie was arriving in two days.

The imminent presence of the woman with whom I had,

more often than not, experienced unpleasantness, provoked in me a wave of anxiety. Doubts about my situation, now stifled by the nervous concentration of waiting, occasionally shed light on what seemed to be a comedy of errors. But I couldn't change my mind. It was impossible not to go pick her up at the airport, not to see her, not to have anything to do with the emotional commitment I had made. I could barely sleep that night, blaming myself violently, getting up to walk around the room in little straight lines within the small rectangle between the desk and the bed. I spent hours trying to avoid making myself even more miserable with the thought that I was awaiting humiliation.

At dawn, I found myself asleep at the table. I went to my bed and fell into it like a huge hulk, disgusted. I spent the rest of that day as if on a tightrope, enveloped in a deceptive calm. My fears had dulled my senses. I was still uneasy but could only half feel it. That night I had the mental space to hope I could be wrong. Maybe, despite my fear, nothing would happen. It wasn't worth thinking about any further, I said to myself, smoking my nth cigarette. I had to go pick her up in the morning.

I saw her before she could catch sight of me amid the crowd. Her hair was again its natural color, but the haircut was different, with the part on the side. She was walking among travelers toward the exit, with steps that seemed too short and slow for her age, carrying a big bag. When she left the terminal, I saw that her eyes were looking for mine. By making a small movement in her direction I attracted her attention, and she ran to embrace me. We stood hugging each other tightly, trying to express the emotion we both needed.

We walked to the taxi station smiling and making prosaic statements about the good old days and about the temperature outside. In letters we had been endlessly eloquent, but now that we were within reach of each other, the mutual presence of our bodies kept us from putting two sentences together. In the taxi, with the city coming into view in the distance, revealing the outlines of its many tall buildings, we held each other's hands and tried to relieve the reality of the silence. It was impossible to find words to say anything, even the obvious.

Arriving at her apartment on Rue de Sèvres was a relief. While Marie paid the taxi driver, I could move away, taking charge of the suitcases. I went up the steps first and opened the door. I let her enter the place she had abandoned months ago and went down to get the rest of the luggage. When I came back up, I told her I had bought some basic food items, including tea. I saw her move, like an old lady, toward the stove.

"And so?" I asked without being able to restrain myself any further.

"Well, as you can see. I'm back. I hope it's all okay."

This felt like a false start. The words weren't going anywhere.

"You don't look bad," she said. "A little thin. Are you still seeing the Pétrements?"

"I go several times a week, but lately it hasn't been so exciting."

"Before, you were enthusiastic."

"I know, but the work has become monotonous. Basically it's like any other. There's no doubt that Didier is a great guy and has been very generous with me, but I don't know, I'm a little fed up."

"Have you seen Sandrine?"

"Not much lately. I suppose she's okay."

Marie brought over the cups and a package of biscuits.

"Thanks for the tea," she said, "and for everything else."

"It was nothing," I answered, but I knew that she was talking about something else. We took refuge behind the steam from the cups.

"And your friend? What's her name? Simone?"

"We're no longer together."

"Ah, bon!"

"We see each other from time to time. It wasn't a breakup, but rather a gradual separation, but that's the end."

"I'm sorry."

"Me too. And you?"

"What?"

"Are you with someone?"

"No. Not right now."

"Why's that?"

"Believe me, it wasn't the moment . . ."

"And how are you doing? I mean, obviously . . ."

"Better. Really much better, though at times I just don't know what the problem is. But I had to return. I couldn't stay there with my parents. And you know how mother is. What she did wasn't right, even though she thought it was for my good. I'm no longer a child."

"What are you going to do now?"

"I don't know yet. For the moment, come back here to live. It's possible that I might take some more classes but not till next year. I have to find a psychiatrist or an analyst. Mom got in touch with her contacts and I already have a few phone numbers, but I'd like to find someone on my own. I still have to figure some things out, to sort out what happened."

We drank our tea in a silence that was no longer anxiety ridden.

"I am so grateful to you for what you've done for me," she said. "Your patience and your understanding. I know that you didn't have to do it. I had no right to expect it of you. I behaved very badly with you. And with others."

"I did it because I wanted to."

"I know. That's why I am asking you to forgive me."

For the first time since her arrival we looked at each other without feeling defensive.

"What do you want to do?" I asked.

"Go to bed with you."

It was a rediscovery. I returned to a body I had not forgotten. The room we were in had witnessed so much misery that, despite the surrender with which we possessed one another, a patina of regrets remained. But it was preferable to ignore or rather to live with it, as if it were an illness, an incurable disease. In our mouths and hands, in the action of our muscles, there was something, despite everything, that retained a perverse, wilted flavor. After the act, when we cavorted with our legs entwined, on the verge of being overtaken by sleep, a poem by Ezra Pound came to my mind, as a kind of warning. Some time later I looked for it. Titled "Fratres Minores," it said: "With minds still hovering above their testicles / Certain poets here and in France / Still sigh over established and natural fact / Long since discussed by Ovid. / They howl. They complain in delicate and exhausted metres / That the twitching of three abdominal nerves / Is incapable of producing a lasting Nirvana."

We went down to have lunch at a fairly good restaurant. It was a bit late in the day and there were only a few customers. I remember I ordered a fish soup, Provençal-style. Through the windows flowed an afternoon whose yellow light was delicate. I could let myself feel the beauty of a Paris where passersby strolled unhurriedly. It felt good to be there. It felt good because I could remember my country and knew that there I would have found none of this: not the soup nor the people nor the extraordinary light nor the woman who faced me and who spoke to me as if nothing had happened between us could be on the streets of the city where I had grown up. Paris became a dream city again, the city it could sometimes be, when one could deal with loneliness and distance.

Slowly, cautiously, more out of habit than anything else, trying to convince myself that I wasn't making a stupid mistake, I returned to Marie. We spent days talking, moving from the table to the bed, or from the bed to the street, from a crêperie to a movie theater, from the movie theater to a walk, or to sitting outside at a café. Our respective studios eliminated any sense of property boundaries between us and we could go to bed and wake up in either of them. Our days and hours were once again richly filled with games and complicities, set aside for so long. I had the impression that the Marie of the previous year had been an aberration, and yet I feared, with equal force, that this new life was a fantasy.

For over a week I devoted myself to her and did not go to work with Didier Pétrement. I had called to let him know the reason for my absence and he and Son kindly invited us to come to dinner. Simone had never wanted to go. She hadn't been interested, didn't feel comfortable in that world, and, rudely, had refused to come for even one visit.

At nightfall, Marie and I took the metro to Didier and Son's house. Before we went in, Marie stopped at a pastry shop to buy raspberry tarts.

From the very first minute, she felt at ease. She chatted and made herself at home in the kitchen with Son while I talked with Didier in the study. We enjoyed a Vietnamese dinner with many dishes, and our conversation lasted as late as possible, until we had to run to the station to catch the last metro. While the women were clearing the plates and preparing herbal tea, Didier took me aside and, as he lit his pipe, blowing big puffs of smoke, he congratulated me on Marie. He was completely enchanted.

From that day on, there were many occasions when, after

I'd spend the afternoon working with Didier, Marie would arrive at the couple's house to prepare dinner with Son, or she
would make us hurry to get to a movie in time, or a lecture
with slides, given by some scholar who had lost himself in
jungles or deserts. Marie even became interested in the work
of Le Petit Vietnamien and read a long series of books Son lent
to her. Her growing interest led her to meditation, and she
considered the possibility of spending the next summer with
me at Monsieur Nan's Swiss community.

Everything seemed to be going wonderfully. Around that
time, Marie's mother traveled to the city and was favorably
impressed with her daughter's progress. For once, finally, she
was pleasant and even showed some affection for me. Nevertheless, despite all the displays of happiness and peace of
mind, something in me still held back from trusting Marie.
I had no reason to, apparently. It seemed to be an irrational
fear, disconnected from actual events, but the truth was that
I couldn't shake this insidious feeling. I was affectionate with
Marie; I needed her complicit presence, her companionship;
I enjoyed what we did and dreamed, but I remained alert, uneasy about a future I couldn't envision.

My research interests were taking shape as a dissertation
project. I worked with discipline and enthusiasm. I imagined
returning to register at the university to earn another degree.
Perhaps ethnology? Continuing to study was the way not to
return to my country, a way to gain time to see if, in some way,
I could remain in France. The city was, then, my world, and
I wouldn't have been surprised or displeased if anyone pre-
dicted that I would stay there.

One day, crossing Place Monge, I ran into Simone. Her hair
was longer, and I realized, upon hugging her, that I had practically never seen her dressed in warm clothing. Somewhat
self-consciously, we began a conversation in the square, which
we then moved across to one of the cafés. We talked about

the university where she was taking some course, about her father and cousins; I reminded her, knowing she would never come to get them, that, hidden in a bag in the bottom of the closet at my place, she had left some pieces of clothing and a few books. We quickly recovered our natural way of being together, laughing at each other over things that had happened to us or that we had done.

When we were served our second coffee and Simone was going for her fourth cigarette, I said: "You know, I have fond memories of you. I'm not sure I'm making myself clear. I remember you without any bitterness, without bad feelings." My intention had been, compelled by the joy of seeing her, to communicate my feelings about the time that had been ours, but upon articulating it, I realized I was saying something else. In my words there was something more than my appreciation for the memories. I was declaring my love and, unbeknownst to Simone, comparing and contrasting her with Marie and, for the first time, finally figuring out what was bothering me. No word was innocent, of course, but, unlike other times, neither was there any ill intent in what I said.

"We had a good time," she said, grabbing my hand. "My father always asks after you. He liked you. He always goes around saying that you were a great guy and always reminds me that you were my only boyfriend who was worth the trouble."

"And what do you think?" My smile suggested playfulness and at the same time veiled my feelings.

"In spite of your many defects and a few of mine, I think that Monsieur Georges is right."

I let myself look away toward any point in the square while I felt the light movements of her hand in mine. More than any other gesture, our hands touching expressed our connection.

After a few seconds she asked: "You're with Marie, right?"

"Yes," I said, stifling my doubt and pain.

"That's how it had to be."

"You think so?"

"It was obvious. *Ça va bien?*"

I let go of her hand and readjusted myself in the chair. I didn't want to lie.

"On the surface, everything is going very well. Psychologically, she's much better. We're not living together, but, for all practical purposes, we might as well be."

"So what's the matter?"

"I don't know. Now that I see you, I realize so many things."

"Don't say that."

"Don't get me wrong. That's not what I'm saying, even though I know I'm saying it. I accept, I understand, what happened between us. I'm not asking you if we can get back together again. I admit that I miss you, and that, seeing you now, the distance between us hurts and I feel a knot in my throat. What I mean is that being with Marie always feels like carrying a dead weight, and she doesn't realize it, or doesn't want to. It's the weight of past frustrations and everything that happened between us. Besides, it's as if I know her so well that there is no space for discovery, for a hopeful new life."

"You're getting bored."

"No, it's not that. We get along well. There are many things I like, including how we are in bed. But I know her: I'm afraid this is not going to last, that what I have now is going to fall apart sooner or later, and I don't want to be here then."

"You're afraid of losing her?"

"No, I'm afraid of finding her. Never, except now, here with you, have I been able to say it, but Marie broke something in me. I don't trust her; I know she's going to do it again and, despite the fact that everything seems to be going so well, I don't want to be here with her again, and at the same time I can't leave."

We soon had to say good-bye.

"Can I call you sometime?" I asked. I was seeking an ally for when the disaster occurred.

"Of course."

In front of the café, we hugged good-bye. My hands brushed over places I knew as a path to pleasure and Simone pushed me away, laughing.

The upsetting content of this conversation and the need to live each day with normality made me repress what I admitted to Simone. Marie was continuing to do well, meditating, regularly going to appointments with the psychiatrist, and telling me her dreams. She tried not to upset me more than was strictly necessary, and enjoyed our walks, talks, and lovemaking. Months passed. In June I finished the dissertation seminar and applied myself to advancing my research as much as possible during vacation. Didier was pleased with the work I did and was counting on me for other projects. I'd accompany him on his visits to museum directors and I know that he loved to enter those strongholds flanked with me as his "secretary." Sometimes, when there was nothing much to do, we'd let the hours fly by, poking around bookstores or galleries of primitive and Oriental art. More than once, we ended up at the Jardin des Plantes, sitting on a bench under an immense plantain tree, near the entrance of the zoo, telling each other our life stories. Thus I found out that Son had fragments of machine-gun bullets in her legs and left hip, and that she slept badly. A son she had had with her first husband had died during a bombing and her spouse had not returned from the front. Pétrement, who had been a steadfast bachelor, had become interested in Son, who, fleeing the tragedy, had made it to Saigon and, as she knew some French, obtained work at the administrative offices of the Alliance. One thing led to the next, and Didier ended up marrying her and bringing her to France. Still, there were times when Son would sit before the altar, light the incense, and sing in a low voice to her little boy.

As the weather got warmer and the afternoons longer, I began to see the first disturbing changes in Marie. I'd listen to her talking on the telephone to her mother and I'd watch her become sugary sweet to the point of agreeing to a two-week vacation with her at a spa known for its medicinal waters. Marie had not consulted me. We had not figured out our plans, but I naturally expected that before making any decision, we'd discuss it first.

Almost immediately, gifts began to arrive: articles of clothing, a Sony Walkman, money to buy more nineteenth-century church chairs in an antique store. I knew the logic of bribery and its seductive game of reciprocity. One could sense the mother's tentacles through her generosity, manipulating the situation so that she could take control. Now, as in the past, I passively played along. I would watch Marie open the packages, show off new garments, turning around in front of the mirror and then carrying on long transatlantic conversations. I grew more and more annoyed but dreaded precipitating the end. Marie was heading toward a place where there was no space for me.

The progression was slow but undeniable. Her mood changed. She'd spend the days without knowing what to do, selfishly using me or our friends to distract herself. I was becoming increasingly bitter over her whims and intolerance, the tiny and apparently arbitrary conflicts that always led to useless and endless talk at night, in which the major topics of envy, friction with others, or the meticulous analysis of some unappreciated detail of her body, revealed the steady progress of her anxiety. One morning we had an absurd argument about some dirty dishes; one Sunday, when I couldn't go out because I had to prepare a written text for my thesis director, she said she didn't want to spend the rest of her life with someone who lived only for books. Ironically, she was the one who, in her happiest moments, encouraged my pursuits and urged

me (and I don't doubt her sincerity) to devote myself to research and writing. Her eating habits became obsessive. She'd
spend days devouring goat cheese and dry bread. Or she'd ex-
orbitantly buy numerous cans of asparagus, open three at a
time and, without putting them on a plate or accompanying
them with some condiment, oblivious to everything around
her, she'd keep munching and downing them as if they were
French fries. Before, when she'd go to her therapy sessions,
she'd talk about what she was discovering. Now she didn't say
a word.

These changes couldn't have happened at a worse time. I
was writing the first pages of my thesis, plus the stories and
reviews I was sending to Santiago's journal in Spain, and I
couldn't even withdraw to work in peace. Marie would arrive
with her monologue or a dense silence. She'd spend a while
reading magazines and silly novels, and then I'd feel her eyes
shooting darts at me. She'd interrupt, asking me to open cans
or bottles, and she'd try to initiate conversations that were
going nowhere, which disrupted my work. Everything would
end in a fight, with her grabbing her bag and leaving abruptly.
From the window, I'd watch her disappear in the direction of
Rue de Vaugirard. I'd go to the stove and prepare coffee. Now
unable to work, I'd drink it listening to the radio.

She fled so as not to face what was really going on. On her
wrist was the scar of the knife cut. It was almost a straight line
that could have passed for the mark of any accident, if not for
its location. This hard fact was always there, in view. Marie
had gotten used to talking with her hands together, the palm
of her right hand covering her left wrist. She would wear, besides, various silver and leather bracelets. Hiding it seemed
worse to me than the scar itself, because her motive seemed to
be not vanity but shame. Her mother had suggested that she
take advantage of the already-planned trip to New York to see
a plastic surgeon. It was none of my business, but the fact that

she contemplated the idea of erasing the scar disturbed me. It was a kind of reverse scarring. Marie thus would inscribe her mother's power and will upon her body.

I kept quiet. I wouldn't have explained myself well, and I wouldn't have been heard. I got to the point of preferring that she'd just leave. That way I'd be able to work, without anxiety or distractions.

At the beginning of July she announced the day she was leaving for New York. Afterwards she would go with her family to some vacation spot in Europe. I was faintly invited to the latter, but both of us knew I had to work on my thesis and with Pétrement and that I had no money for travel.

I took her to the airport. A few days before leaving, she had doubts. She wondered if it wouldn't be better, instead, for us to go on a spiritual retreat with Monsieur Nan. We were treating each other better, and the activities we were sharing somewhat recovered the tone of the good times. I even thought that the trip didn't have to lead to catastrophe. All of us have a right to our ups and downs, to lose our way, to err. Perhaps Marie needed a reunion with her mother to reassert herself. We said good-bye in good spirits, promising to write often.

The first days were good. I recovered my space and worked easily and contentedly. Then the solitude began to weigh on me, and I had a hard time filling the hours, even with the lure of work. I exchanged long letters with Santiago and Isabel in which, among other things, we promised to meet up again, either in Alicante or in Paris. Almost a year had passed since we met each other in Spain and the pleasure of our contact was still fresh. But, after all, a reunion depended almost exclusively on my slim resources. Without family and without friends— the Pétrements were traveling and were going to spend some days with Le Petit Vietnamien—I found myself killing time in parts of the city far from my studio, half-exhausted by the heat, flipping through boxes of books on sale in small neighborhood bookstores or looking at the windows of stores that were selling puppets or enamel figurines. I visited many jewelry stores in search of a cheap watch, because the old mechanism in the one my father had given me years ago had stopped. I'd check out, while walking or sitting on park benches, the bustling of the tourists and the beauty of the women coming to the city from all over the globe. I surrendered, like Parisians who couldn't travel, to the irritating noise of their happiness.

I received brief, anecdotal letters from Marie, in which she told me about her theater and opera outings, about the weekends spent at the beach house, or a dinner in a luxurious Russian restaurant, in which her father got so drunk that he hired a band of Gypsy musicians. In my room I'd answer her, writing on the pinewood desk that was stained with ink, paint, wine, and coffee. It pleased me to leave these traces of my existence, which little by little were becoming a palimpsest. Paris was teaching me to discover minimal beauty, to honor these findings as a way of validating life.

One evening, after the postman's second visit, I found a letter from Marie that filled less than one page. It contained two pieces of news. She said that she couldn't write anymore because she had a lot of pain from the surgery, and that in three days she was leaving with her parents for Portugal. She would write again when she had recovered and knew her new address. The brevity of this bulletin left me uneasy. I felt sure that she had gone too far and that everything was about to fall apart. It was useless to think that I was fantasizing all this.

The days kept going by without further news of Marie. At some point, I could no longer chalk it up to the post office's inefficiency. Marie, for some reason I didn't know, but whose dark tone I could anticipate, did not want to write to me. I felt a whole range of emotions, ending up with disbelief, anger, and depression. I knew that, somewhere in Europe, Marie was betraying me. My mind fought to reach other conclusions, but my certainty grew stronger and more and more humiliating.

I stopped working on my thesis. I had twenty-four hours of the day to myself, but I couldn't work. I'd waste time on absurd activities, like washing the worn-out rug in the studio with my hands or throwing a ball made of socks in the air, again and again. I grew so desperate that I went to see Sandrine to ask her point-blank if she knew anything about her friend. When she showed me the postcard from Portugal written in a hotel in the Algarve, the news hit me like a punch in the face. As I walked out, I felt as if molten lead had been poured inside me. Once again, with my fear of loneliness, I had created my own personal form of hell.

This time, I didn't even feel like walking. I dragged my feet to an anonymous café in the Fifteenth arrondissement, where I had only been once before, soon after arriving in the city. At that time I spoke very bad French and I remembered, as I sat at one of the tables, how difficult it was to order anything when my accent was almost incomprehensible and I didn't recognize most of the dishes. A long history separated me from those days. The city and its culture had shaped me, and I had found here a space for my life's labors. It was difficult to imagine living somewhere else than this world of pedestrians inhabiting the city as if it were an extension of their apartments. But that afternoon, in that café, I suddenly thought of returning. Nothing, nobody, now was keeping me from returning home. I needed to decide where home was, though, since up until that moment, mine was in the Impasse de l'Astrolabe. Over there, far away, was the island I came from. I never denied it; it had always been my hallmark of identity. I had always defended Puerto Rico in a world that didn't care to know us. But I knew it was a hole in the wall, and that very little of what was done in Paris could be reproduced in my native city. But I couldn't take it anymore. I had no more strength to continue fighting, and even more significant, I didn't feel strong enough to be near Marie. Being lonely and poor didn't help, but Marie was, so to speak, the straw that broke the camel's back. In that café, during the hour and half I spent there, the notion that my time in the city had come to an end, quietly took root in me. It was like an epiphany, produced by a contradictory rush of emotions: failure, hope, and willpower all rolled into one compelling impulse.

Night and dawn found me on the streets and boulevards of the city, struggling with a decision I'd already made but couldn't quite swallow. Between the bridges of the Seine and the stairs of Saint-Sulpice, I walked, rehearsing countless versions of a single thought. I suffered the pain and indignity of abandonment. The city had been mine, but its people had not. I came to realize this, walking along the dark gates of the Luxembourg Gardens or watching the crowds pour out of the movie theaters on Boulevard du Montparnasse. I couldn't continue living as if I were reading a book. My world had been made of paper, and in it the humans, the French, had been held at a thoughtless distance. This was the flip side of the story of those years. It's possible that at certain ages one comes to earth-shattering realizations. It is possible, because that night I recognized that I had no choice but to return.

I couldn't entirely justify, in words, my decision to leave Paris. It was something I will never be able to completely understand—perhaps associated with the lost and eternal world of childhood. The limitations of my life with Marie were also perhaps the sign of another point of no return. I will never be able to explain satisfactorily why I left the city. I left, in fact, because I couldn't explain it.

The next day I got up late and, amazingly, my resolution was still firm. Daylight, the streets, the people had a unique lightness or lack that was a liberating release from some great weight. I called San Juan. My family agreed to send money for the flight and for the trunk that I would send by ship. I didn't want to visualize what awaited me. I had made a decision I could not undo. In the following two weeks I sold what I could and went to meet with my thesis director, who tried to convince me that when I found myself back in San Juan, I would realize the magnitude of my error. Before a few final chores, since there were still a few days remaining before my trip, I went to Marie's apartment and left off a letter in which I asked her to return my studio key to the landlord, thus terminating the rental. At the end there was a good-bye without any explanation. I spent several days free of all tasks and obligations, living in a room with only a mattress and a pile of clothing and a few random things.

I called Simone and we made a date to meet at a café. I spoke for quite a while before giving her the news. She was sensible enough not to try and poke her nose into my life, but she invited me to her house one more time, presumably because her father wanted to say good-bye.

I came with two bottles of strong wine from Algeria. We all prepared the food together, as we always had, and consumed it at a leisurely pace, engrossed in a conversation mixed with joy, nostalgia, and heartbreak. There was a momentous toast by Simone's father, in which he expressed all his feelings, from the sadness that my departure inspired to a drunken and disillusioned climax about not having me as a son-in-law. When it was late, and we had no hope of catching the last train, Georges fell asleep in his chair and Simone took me to her room, where we made love and talked until it began to get light outside the windows. I got dressed, as I wanted to leave before breakfast. After those hours with her, she was playing at unraveling my plan to leave. I realized how much I loved her, but I knew that she would not fill the void compelling me to leave the city. I should not hold onto anyone.

Wrapped in a sweater, Simone accompanied me to the staircase landing. Our embrace left us looking at each other with teary eyes. I heard her voice cracking when I reached the front door to the building. "Bon chance!" She was wishing me good luck as if I were going to an exam.

Sometime later I would find out, in one of her letters, that at that time she was going out with a man who would abandon her when she became pregnant.

I purposely left the visit to the Pétrements for one of the last days before my departure. I knew that if anyone could change my mind, that person would be Didier. Conscious of this, I told him of my decision in front of Son. I thought that her presence would soften his reaction. Didier stood up and turned his back to me.

"You've gone completely crazy." It was the first time he addressed me as *tu* in the familiar form. "A man doesn't put himself through such things for women."

"Didier," Son interceded, "please, don't be so rude."

"So, can you tell me why this fool is going?"

"Because he has to go. That's all. The French don't understand this."

"There's nothing to understand. Why do you come here today to present us with a done deed? Why didn't you come before, to consult me?"

"Because he knew that you were going to give him this speech," said Son. "That you were going to turn into some sort of horrible father."

Didier made an irritated gesture while he lit his pipe. He walked around his office avoiding the piles of books and papers until he stood facing the window.

"It's what always happens," he said. "Nothing lasts. You, after all, must be master of your own mistakes, your own stupidities. Forgive me for saying it like that. Tell me if there is something we can do to change your mind."

"There's nothing to be done, Didier," I said. "I must go."

The light coming in the window gave the smoke surrounding his shoulders a bluish density. We remained in silence for a long time; then we watched him go over to a cabinet, take out a bottle and three glasses.

"Perhaps you're right. Perhaps you're both right, even though you're the biggest fool I've known in my life. But it doesn't matter anymore. Go home knowing that Son and I are your friends."

Son came over to kiss me and Didier gave me a hug that made my spine creak.

In the little time I had left in the city I saw them twice. We dined, had lunch, walked, and let the hours pass chatting about any old thing at a café table.

The day of my departure, I took the baggage and suitcases downstairs and gave the mailbox one last look. There was nothing. I got into the taxi and we went along the boulevards before getting on the highway. I was leaving everything I had come to find. Maybe this was nothing, but it had a tremendous weight.

After handing them my luggage at the airlines counter, I bought, with my last francs, a few packages of Gauloises and walked toward the gates. I sat on a bench and waited a little over a half hour watching the passengers move around. I wanted to savor the very last drop of France. When I saw that it was already time to board, I stood up, feeling my nerves tightening in my stomach.

Then, unexpectedly, I ran into Didier and Son.

"Tiens, mon vieux, c'est pour toi."

My companion of so many days had placed a package in my hands.

"Don't forget us," said Son.

After passing through security, I walked backwards, until I lost sight of them.

I opened the package a few minutes after the plane took off. It contained the first slightly faded edition of Pierre Plon's translations of myths and songs. On the first page there was a dedication. It said: "To Didier Pétrement with whom I lived the greatest years of my life."

SAN JUAN

1

San Juan received me as a stranger. I had spent over nine years outside the country, only visiting for brief periods. Since I'd left college, my life had been organized around foreign countries. I wanted to make the most of my time abroad and, whenever I had breaks or vacations, had tried not to spend them in San Juan. Besides—and I didn't admit this for a long time—I was afraid of this city. I knew too well the limits it imposed on the sort of life I had sought far away. The truth was that, while I'd been defending my home culture with convoluted arguments and mythmaking, trying to fend off the feeling of being a whole continent away, in reality, I hated too many things about life here. San Juan was my city, the place where I belonged more than any other. I didn't doubt it, but this belonging could feel like a cruel bond, a chain forged by an accident of birth, or bad luck.

Aside from my family, I knew only a few friends from my college years, and (except for short trips to foreign countries) they had always lived in Puerto Rico. They held modest jobs. They were schoolteachers, bureaucrats, technicians. Some were studying endlessly for a PhD. What we had in common and what led me back to them was that they were all readers. As they had nothing to do with business and didn't practice any high-paying profession, they were pleasantly marginal.

The country was suffocating. This was not news: I could tell from the very moment I arrived. The porter at the airport spoke to me in English and tried to cheat me. Through a crack in the paper they'd pasted on the terminal windows, making them a blind wall, I searched for my parents. I found them looking lost in a noisy, sweaty crowd who dressed, pushed, and shouted in a way that suddenly turned the scene, for me, into a nightmare memory. To the world I had just left behind, we were a caricature, a joke. We lived amid small ideas and trivial work, in an insular world of fantasy. I would quickly discover that my interests were met with nasty, belittling expressions of contempt, like, "So what?" or "Who cares?" This was why I had left, tired of a society that sentenced me to eccentricity and isolation. Politically, we were the same old disaster, aggravated at that time by the vulgarity and violence of the Romero government, which seemed to speak its own dialect, barely comprehensible to others. Its rhetoric was plagued with unexpected pauses, interjections, whole sections of orations that devolved into some sort of raving, which most people, totally uninterested, listened to with the routine resignation of watching the rain.

I remember my first days, my hopeful reencounter with the city, which in spite of everything, I still missed. I took a walk around the old town, stopping by its arts and crafts shops, its art galleries, and its bars. I remember my perhaps excessive enthusiasm on discovering the carnival masks of Ponce, the wooden saints, coffee cups made with coconut shells, or finding, in the corner of the inner patio of a gallery, abstract textiles from a tribe in the Sahara and wicker bowls from Zimbabwe.

In my last days in Paris, I had struggled with a deep-seated loneliness, a feeling of bereft orphanhood, of lost origins. Being abandoned by Marie had intensified this underlying homesickness. So in returning to Puerto Rico, I wasn't just running away. Hope and youth convinced me I could begin again, and that I could make use, here, of what I had learned abroad.

Soon these aspirations clashed with reality. Their provincialism made it impossible for people to understand my situation. I was one of thousands of students who left to study abroad, but for most Puerto Ricans, the world beyond the island was almost exclusively the United States. Going to France was interesting in principle, but once they considered what I had had to live through, only to return without either a degree or fortune, the experience seemed an incomprehensible waste. I got tired of being constantly asked where I was from. Annoyed, I'd always reply, "From here," only to encounter the tribal disbelief of my interrogator. Talking to anybody about the things I devoted myself to in France meant sounding unintelligible. What could Amazonian culture, Tibetan art, or modern art and narrative mean here? What unimaginable assumptions would they make about me, listening to my way of speaking, now that I had lost the tics of the local accent in those years away?

I'd spend the days in my family home, discussing the news of the day with my mother, reading, rediscovering the taste and aroma of a coffee that was so unlike the disgusting brews I had sipped for years. Almost everyday, in the afternoons, I'd go out for a walk in a city where people no longer walked. I'd walk along awful avenues that were hostile to pedestrians, like Roosevelt or Central, without anything to enjoy looking at except signs, cars, posts, cracks in the cement. Sometimes I'd end up in a pastry shop, which was the closest thing to a Parisian café in San Juan, and spend hours watching and smoking, as if I couldn't fully believe the reality before my eyes.

At night my father would lend me his car and I'd go to see my friends. I'd hang out in the small living rooms of their apartments or, if it was Thursday, Friday or Saturday, in some bar or restaurant. Sometimes we'd go to the movies; sometimes there was absolutely nothing to see, and we'd sit there bored in front of our beers until our yawns forced me to say good night.

When I felt like it, I'd take a ride around the city. I'd go around the barrios with their deserted sidewalks: Santurce,

Miramar, El Condado, Ocean Park, Puntas las Marías, Isla Verde. My mind would travel, too. I saw myself inhabiting some of the balconies that still had lights on in the early hours of the morning, and I imagined the cool, refreshing sea breeze, the joy I'd feel from cloudbursts, from reading in the low light with the balcony doors opened, from the arrival of old and new friends. I would live here, and perhaps the years spent far away would serve some purpose. It was a pleasant fantasy and a way of accepting the decision I had made. It had the grace of a certain peace, of some sort of relief. On other occasions I imagined myself, after many years, living on the top floor of a rundown old building in Santurce. There, isolated and forgotten, I would write the novel about this city, which would justify my existence. I didn't know then that for years and years I would stick to this course of action and fantasy, ultimately inseparable (in my mind) from the city itself.

A few weeks after my arrival, I got a part-time job at a language academy. I would give private lessons in Spanish to North Americans sent by their companies to work on the island. A bit later, I was able to complement these earnings with a class at the Alliance Française. My work was unbearably humdrum. Nothing in my education prepared me for teaching languages, and the incessant repetition and correction of absurdly simple sentences bored me to death. I began trying to connect with new acquaintances here and soon realized that the assumptions I would bring to conversations did not work at all. I couldn't presume that these people knew anything about anything, that they knew an author, a historical event, the geographical setting of a country, or that they even had the slightest curiosity to find out about these things. Nonetheless, they were mostly good people, satisfied with the certainties that were sufficient for living here. However, it was hard for me to feel at ease. I had the impression that I was almost always concealing large parts of myself and that little by little I was constructing an identity based on suppression. For years I had practiced in my mind foreign phrases before uttering them, and now, continually, I was choosing to translate what I wanted to express into what I assumed they were ready to hear. In both cases much was lost. In both cases, I felt an insidious loneliness.

At the Alliance I taught a handful of French people who had come to San Juan mostly because they were married to Puerto Ricans. The interest and liberalism toward other cultures that one finds in Paris, at least intellectually, had eroded in them once they had lived in Puerto Rico. I witnessed a lot of grandiloquent posturing, punctuated by prejudice and lack of understanding, which made of their lives—except for time on the beaches and their annual trip to their cities in France—a kind of prison sentence on Devil's Island. I could understand what they were experiencing, but their colonialist airs set me against them. At the beginning, they'd invite me to their parties and get-togethers, which, after the wine and delicious hors d'oeuvres, would turn into assemblies of a white fraternity. Here people would speak of what was missed by living far from France, and one would end up attending heated discussions in which they ranted against almost everything about this country. A horrible complicity reigned among the French and their spouses and most of the Puerto Rican fauna swarming in these Europeanizing venues, in which one accepted with a dignity at once shy and awkward the devastating critique of those judgmental stares. Far from this country, I had always defended my belonging here. I always thought we had a history, a culture upon which to stand firm, with which to validate our existence. I suddenly found myself alone, or in a minority, defending positions of which most of my compatriots weren't even aware. I saw them bow their heads and agree with the French. I think that, around that time, I first heard the current usage of the term *puertorriqueñidad*, or "Puerto

Ricanness." The term arose, in part, in response to the belief that it was culturally glamorous to imagine not being Puerto Rican.

Most of the students of the Alliance were middle-aged *sanjuaneros* who went to French class as others went to play golf on Saturdays. They had an idyllic vision of France, which most of the time didn't go beyond a grand tour of monuments with wine and cheese tastings. I was teaching an advanced conversation class in which I had to prepare exercises like sample conversations between a waiter in a café and a tourist. One day I decided we would base a conversation on literature, on something we had read. The group hated this so much that they went to complain to the director. I was called into his office, decorated with posters of tourist sites and big exhibits at the Louvre or the Grand Palais, and after being offered a cigarette by one of the few smokers of Gitanes in the country, I had to listen to a lecture on how our students had to be entertained by learning about a universal language and culture. This wasn't a university, he said, and we have to limit ourselves to teaching them proper pronunciation.

His argument placed me in a difficult situation. He was the headmaster of the Alliance and as such I had to submit to his rules, like them or not. But on the other hand, I felt attacked by his paternalism. The conversation quickly turned into an argument and the next semester there were no courses for me.

The result of this contretemps would have been hard for me to imagine back in Paris. From then on I lived without practically any connection to French culture or to the French people. In Puerto Rico there were barely any books to be had, and little by little, I went through the two or three hundred titles I had brought with me. The same thing happened with music or other areas of culture. I didn't have, and wouldn't for a long time, a penny to my name, and interest in all things French here was about money, not culture, and implied a certain social position. All this had very little to do with the Paris I had known. The French and Francophile types who gathered in this part of the world ceased to interest me. France faded slowly into the horizon. I stopped speaking the language altogether (I didn't have anyone to speak it with). There are people who have known me here for years and who haven't the slightest notion that I speak French.

After living with my parents for some time, I looked for my own place. I'd walk around old San Juan to see if there were For Rent signs on the balconies. After visiting several that I couldn't afford, I ended up putting down a deposit on an apartment that was very small but had, like many houses in this area, very high ceilings, underneath which they had built a wooden loft space which served as a bedroom. The place was hot and slightly claustrophobic, and on the weekends it didn't keep out the racket from the street, but for the time being, it worked for me. I brought my belongings from my parents' house and acquired something I'd never managed to possess in the countless rooms I'd lived in: a telephone.

I got around by bus until I accepted my father's generosity and bought a used Datsun. My friends would come to visit me Friday nights. We'd talk about books, politics, or whatever the hours and the rum would bring. Their presence was very pleasant but did not hide the fact that I was still alone. Many things hadn't gelled in my life, and it was impossible for me, then, to do away with the expectations surrounding my return. I was living here, but this *here* was not what I had imagined from a distance and expected to discover upon landing in the city. The disappointment was painful and incomprehensible. I was too young to understand this misery.

I've thought that the story of a person like myself could be expressed by chronicling the books and music that memory preserves from each era of one's life. It strikes me that upon picking up a volume or listening to a melody, one reproduces in miniature the famous Proustian scene. Those first years in San Juan could be Salvador Elizondo's *El grafógrafo*, or Emilio Díaz Valcárcel's *Schemes in the Month of March* or the anthologies of stories from the seventies generation or Juan José Saer's *The Witness* or a rereading of Juan Carlos Onetti's *The Brief Life* or a newly arrived copy of José Donoso's *Curfew*. In those days I read Manuel Ramos Otero, and José Luis Gonzalez was still alive. I didn't even have to read those books from beginning to end; the mere intention to read them already said the whole story. How often did I go to the bookstores, like the little one on San José street, opened even on Sundays, to stop at the table of new books; how often did I spend Saturday afternoons in Río Piedras between the basement of La Tertulia and the labyrinth of the Hispanoamericana? In these memories my emotions still stir, from the pleasurable expectation of seeing a new title to the sadness that inspires so much reading. I can say the same for the sounds of Roy Brown and Aires Bucaneros, Silvio Rodríguez and Pablo Milanés, of some record still on vinyl of Andrés Jiménez, Rubén Blades, Willy Colón, and from the political and cultural airs coming from Cuba, Nicaragua, and the rest of Latin America. There still remained some hope, some freshness in my life and one could still sip a bit of it at the bars and café nightclubs. The world could still change with a bottle of rum and the right tune.

It was around that time, a few months after I'd returned, the first letters arrived from Paris. The Pétrements and Simone wrote several pages filled with nostalgia and good wishes, but one day I found in my mailbox the letter that I know sooner or later would reach me. Just by feeling its weight and seeing Marie's nervous, minuscule script—somehow she had gotten my new address—I knew it would be long and difficult to read.

At the beginning her tone was dry and bitter. She wrote out of indignation and guilt, and this irreconcilable mixture made her proceed in fits and starts. She said that even taking into consideration her role in the drama, she felt my reaction was absurd. She had never imagined that, on her return, she would find not only my terse letter but also that I had gone. There was no excuse, she said, for this hostility. It was ridiculous to throw overboard so much effort, to destroy without a second thought the future I was forging in Paris. In any case, the consequences of my actions were ultimately my problem; however, my departure also had an effect on her. According to Marie, nothing of what she had done had justified such a breakup. It was true she hadn't written to me until now, which wasn't right either. She admitted that. As I had doubtlessly presumed, she had gotten involved in a meaningless relationship with some man, but she felt I had reacted with a ferocity that the situation didn't merit. We had survived such things before, and we would have been able to survive this too. She had fallen into a period of confusion that, unfortunately, had hurt me. For this she was responsible, but for the rest she could not forgive me. And besides, if things didn't work between us, I always could have stayed in Paris and continued with my life. She was worried about what hardships I might be experiencing. She had visited Didier and Son, and they had spent a whole evening talking about me. Didier did not stop repeating, as he served more than half a bottle of cognac, that sooner or later I would feel suffocated in Puerto Rico. She encouraged me to reconsider my actions and to consider returning. I didn't have to see her if I didn't want to, although she wished that I would, but in no way should I be doing this damage to myself. "You must know that I've loved you and that I love you more than anybody, and this has nothing to do with our being together. I hope that you'll forgive me and that I can forgive you, and am sending my love to you, all my love."

I was already filled with doubts about having returned to Puerto Rico, and the letter made them worse. Perhaps I had acted out of an impulsiveness that was not typical of me and had been excessive, but at the time I had felt certain. And I was still sure of my decision. I didn't know why (most probably I couldn't explain it in a convincing way), but this was my reality. I had had to return, even if it was to suffer in this society in which I barely knew myself but which was the only one that could be mine.

I couldn't answer her right away. Many times did I reread those pages with their lines scrunched together, and for a whole week I drafted and revised my answer. When I finally sat down to write, I put on paper only a fraction of what I had composed in my mind. I was capable only of addressing whatever was most anecdotal. The brief time spent in San Juan had diminished my sadness and I was no longer in any mood for arguments. I ended by reiterating my affection and the hope that someday we would meet again on good terms. But for the time being, I was staying put. I needed to be here, and besides, I had nowhere else to go.

Time gradually blurred the past. I lived as best as I could. The reencounter with the country made me return to writing, and the atmosphere of Old San Juan with its galleries and museums, aside from the dead time of loneliness, got me to take up again paints and brushes. With the passing of the years I was becoming another man and got to be many things: artist, teacher, painter and decorator, mediocre carpenter. I lived in many rooms and houses, embarked on and weathered the shipwrecks of several love affairs, and over a decade later finally became a father and husband. I built a life in San Juan, which, if it hasn't been the best, has at least been my destiny. I've had a somewhat gray existence, which perhaps has given me the freedom to abandon many illusions. I expect very little. My motivations and pleasures are simple; achieving them is often precarious. But I have assimilated to this place that is mine in the world.

That is my story. I do not know how much of it is true, or how much I have rationalized my defects and weaknesses. But I do know that coming home to Puerto Rico was more important than all my travels. I don't think it was merely a fleeing, an escape, but that no longer matters. Paris (or any other place) has ceased to be *Paris*. I have no more trips left to take.

San Juan came to be a corrosive acid that erased the past. Sometimes I have a hard time recognizing its faded traces. Memory, or rather the rational role I play in my memories, feels like a novel or movie read or seen years ago. Very little remains to tell, as if life in San Juan didn't allow for having relationships with any other part of the world. After many letters and a surprise visit that resolved nothing and left me even more confused, my relationship with Marie dissolved. This was doubtlessly for the best. Her life kept going in circles around the same old problems. I didn't want to have to deal with that anymore. When I saw her that last time, I did my best to bring her down to earth. To this end, I presented myself as weighed down by all my frustrations. I was a loner, poor and bitter, and didn't pretend to be otherwise. I took her to the places I frequented, mediocre bars, restaurants, and parks that were often also dirty. She saw me get drunk every night while the electric fan, whose grate was covered with rust and dust, swiveled back and forth between us. Successively I tried to elicit her pity, sorrow, guilt, and repulsion, and to provoke the pain of both having lost me and seeing me lost in San Juan. Only bed with her could bring relief to those days. Only there could I breathe without hating her.

After an absence of several years in which we had no contact, I received from her, fairly recently, an absurd and nostalgic letter which I didn't answer. I learned that Sandrine had married, divorced, and married the same man again—and, the last I heard, now lives with another man in Le Mans. Meanwhile, Simone has brought up her child alone, and every once in a great while I receive a postcard from her, almost always from some vacation spot, telling me she's alive, more or less fine, and that she remembers me.

Didier Pétrement died a few months ago. Son sent me the news, and at the same time announced she was returning to Vietnam to live with her sister and nephews in Le Petit Vietnamien's community there. Until the very end, Didier was loyal. We would write to each other regularly, and I always had news of his museum adventures and misadventures. He, in turn, knew about my problems and followed with interest the course of my projects. I would send him my books and catalogs of art shows, and he was sorry that his knowledge of languages didn't include Spanish. Nevertheless, I am sure that he was the best reader I had. Then again, there haven't been many, but rather a vast throng of readers who have never read me.

Since the time I left Paris, Didier and I were resigned to the fact that our relationship would not have the intensity it had before. Always, when I wrote to him, I *translated* my life; I would change things in these narratives so that he could understand and accept them without getting furious. We had a way of dealing with each other that we maintained until the end, unspoken. This was a way of making our affection for each other survive; it was a way to eliminate the penalty imposed by distance.

I felt reduced, impoverished by his death, but also freer. It became easier to live here, to be whoever I was on these streets, the person I might have never accepted otherwise. Sometimes I still light up incense sticks and think of him, remembering his dimly lit, encyclopedic workplace, seeing myself next to the hulk of his body, while he was showing me images and telling me things (myths, histories, archeological scandals) which were perhaps the most important stories I've heard in my life.

After an almost endless process (which I was on the verge of abandoning on numerous occasions) I finished my thesis. I spent a year and a half without a job, sometimes painting houses or cleaning pools, before attaining a contract at the University of Puerto Rico. I've been teaching there for over a decade, and I try to emulate some of the rigor and passion of my former teachers.

But, after leaving Paris and before becoming a university professor, I was a Spanish teacher at a private high school. That was my first job with a regular salary and the first time I had the opportunity to practice what I had studied. I labored there, like any novice anxious to prove himself, with exaggerated energy and enthusiasm. The willpower I put into my classes gradually tamed the students' lack of discipline and awakened their interest. I was just a few years older than the seniors, and because I played basketball with them and went to their parties as well as teaching them, an atmosphere of camaraderie developed among us. During our Friday class, they'd ask me to talk about Paris. It was a way of relaxing the rigorous classroom atmosphere, but also a way to get to know each other. They were no doubt expecting the tale of my affairs with the women (whom they imagined excitingly liberal) but instead they got—and they began to listen more closely and seriously—the story of what my life had been there. When the hour was ending, promising more chapters, I discovered in them something akin to a kind of vague hope. Perhaps this was the first time they realized that, aside from following the business or professional paths of their fathers, there existed, for whoever wished to take them, other paths. It was in this way that Alejandro Espinal learned of me.

One night, after eating with some friends, I parked in the high part of the city. I was still living in Old San Juan, but I had moved to an apartment on Calle Cruz. This fascinated my students since it was the neighborhood where they hung out, and they assumed that, living so close to the bars, my life

would be a kind of endless party. At some point I had mentioned the street where I lived without going into details, as I
didn't want them visiting me at all hours of the day or night.
I was walking down the deserted slope of the road when I noticed a couple further ahead. They were shouting something,
looking up. This was a common scene in San Juan, as most of
the buildings didn't have doorbells, so visitors had to shout
to announce their arrival. I didn't pay any further attention to
them until I got to the entrance and started to struggle with
the lock. The couple was shouting my name. The boy was
blondish, thin, and wore glasses; his companion was an attrac-
tive light-skinned black girl who was slightly plump. I waited;
they saw I was looking at them and shouted again.

"Who are you looking for?" I asked.

They said my name, my occupation, and the place where I
worked.

"That's me," I said, surprised.

They came over to me, laughing. They had been looking for
me for three nights and had shouted my name time and again
at all the buildings on Calle Cruz, and—pointlessly—on the
adjacent street, Calle Justo. They had followed my classes from
afar, because they had heard about them from a friend, and
had decided to meet me. I had made my students read great
writing such as Cortázar's *Hopscotch*, Vallejo's poetry, stories
by Carpentier and Borges. I had playfully introduced them
to the *nivolas* of Unamuno and had acquainted them with a
group of new Puerto Rican writers—Rodríguez Juliá, Ramos
Otero, Magali García Ramis, Ana Lydia Vega—in whom they
discovered an intimate, lively world they had never seen or
imagined could be conjured up so well in a book. The story
of their search for me was incredible. Alejandro Espinal was a
friend of Guillermo Fernández, one of my best students, the
only one who said he wanted to be an artist, and who was constantly drawing, reading, and writing. Alejandro had left high

school before beginning his senior year because, according to what he said that night, he couldn't stand being in all-boy classes or the oppressive atmosphere of future technocrats. At this point he was finishing college in the public system and, as was natural, he was still hanging out with some of his old high school friends. Thus he knew about my stories of Paris and wanted to meet me because he too wanted to go to France. The girl was smiling and nodding as Alejandro spoke rapidly, the words tumbling out of his mouth, his manner shy and at the same time arrogant.

I was captivated by his determination to make my acquaintance, and so that our meeting wouldn't be so brief, I invited them for a beer. We went up the hill toward the bar Hijos de Borinquen which was then on San José Street, on the corner of Luna. I liked its unpretentious atmosphere and its hybrid nature (it was a mixture of bar and grocery store), and because it sold natural juices and had a jukebox that played the best Puerto Rican and Caribbean music. We found a table and I ordered three Medalla beers from the skinny old waiter.

We spoke about school and his former classmates. Alejandro gave terse answers, as if he weren't interested in the direction the conversation was taking. He smoked nervously and laughed with the girl about things I didn't understand. He mentioned Paris, trying to get me to talk about the city. I didn't feel like it. He was very young, and I knew that his dreams would soon vanish for the most ordinary reasons. Besides, I had returned, Paris felt far away, and the reasons I had left did not form part of my best memories. I didn't get that Alejandro had sought me out for days because of the attractions that Paris held for him. It didn't pique my vanity that someone wanted to follow in my footsteps. I knew from experience that following such dreams of travel could be a mistake.

After a while, I made an excuse about having to get up early. With nothing more to talk about, they accompanied me to the door of my house. I didn't invite them in, or to come visit me sometime. I congratulated them for finding me and said good-bye assuming I would never see them again.

We cannot always know what certain encounters may bring into our lives. There are people who don't know who they really are or their effect on others. This significance is beyond them and they become the bearers of a message they don't even know they convey. Alejandro Espinal would bring to me the most destructive and most lucid silence. His life would become a territory through which my days would blindly pass. He was only a detail, a short chain of incidents, but in him, more than in many events of my biography, lingered the danger of San Juan. He forced me to see what I never wanted to see. The society I lived in had also avoided contact, for centuries, with this image of itself. Unconsciously, my time in San Juan became a battle with the fast-moving shadow of Alejandro's history.

I didn't last much longer at the prep school. My innovations in the curriculum sparked controversies, and the shadowy and manipulative moves by the priests provoked uneasiness among the professors who had now chosen me to represent them. One day the director called me to his office and showed me evaluations of my classes. This document was unusual, as nobody had come to observe them. I knew what this consultation meant: when the year ended, they would not renew my contract. I decided to hand in my resignation after Christmas. I thought it was better to focus on my thesis than to wait and be left without a job. My parents helped me out financially, and seven or eight months later, I sent the manuscript to my director. At the end of October, I traveled to Paris for my defense. I stayed at Didier and Son's house. I didn't have to resist the temptation to get in touch with Marie because she had returned to live with her parents in New York, but I had a brief encounter with Sandrine. Time had distanced us, and our dinner in a restaurant was excruciatingly dull.

I planned to leave Simone in peace with her new partner, but after a few days with the Pétrements, the temptation was too great, and I called her. We met at the Café de l'Arrivée, almost directly facing the train station at Montparnasse. She was the same as ever, and the joy of seeing each other led us to rent a room in a rather dubious hotel, which we didn't leave except to buy *merguez* sausage sandwiches at an Arab stand. We spent the whole night without sleeping, just talking and making love. When I returned the next morning, Didier and Son, who had noticed my absence, asked where I had been and, before falling into a deep sleep, I told them about my long coffee date with Simone. Before I left Paris, she and I decided, on a couple of occasions, to spend the whole night again in those labyrinths in which down-and-out traveling salesmen would give free rein to their secret desires.

I defended my thesis during a strike at the university. My director and I entered the Sorbonne through a side door that the students hadn't barricaded. I presented my work without the attendance of a defense committee, when the building was completely deserted and the shouting of the protesters could be heard in the background. At the end, the director left his approval letter signed on the desk of an absent departmental chair. It would take me a long time to get hold of the diploma that officially documented my PhD. Afterwards, we left by the same door we'd entered, and in front of the metro station, I received the embrace that sealed the completion of my studies.

I walked a while around the neighborhood of the Place de la Contrescarpe and Rue Descartes feeling that the whole thing was a joke in poor taste. The end of my odyssey was strikingly banal: the signing of a piece of paper while sitting in an empty office.

Melancholy and the cold evening air eventually drove me to enter the metro and return to the Pétrements, who awaited me to go and celebrate in a restaurant.

Shortly after this, I left on a train for Alicante. Santiago and Isabel had invited me to spend a few days with them. Autumn had transformed the Spanish landscape, and the city was deserted and a bit gloomy. The color of the sea, once impeccably blue, had now turned gray, and a wind coming from the east chilled us to the bone. Amid dinners and excursions, I considered the possibility of staying there. My life in San Juan was lonely and unrewarding. Here I had the warmth of friendship and a world that offered some novelty. With a little persistence, I could find work as a translator or as an English teacher. But one evening Santiago made me see the light. I had no papers and I had never worked in Spain. Nor was I really attracted to the prospect of spending my life translating business documents or teaching the rudiments of a language. In San Juan, things might change once I had the doctorate in hand. After two weeks I hugged my friends good-bye at the railroad station. I spent a night in Madrid and took the midnight flight to San Juan.

I arrived on the morning of December 24. Weeks of absence had left an impressive layer of dust and salt residue on all the surfaces of the apartment. I spent the days of that Christmas break reading the books by Neptune I had bought in Paris. I'd had a hard time finding some of them. They were the first and only editions of an unclassifiable literature, the kind that didn't fit in any genre. The covers and pages had already begun to turn yellow. It was instructive to consider this fact. Even in a literary city, a writer like Neptune could be obscure and his books practically unattainable. What could one expect in Puerto Rico, where much of the best literature died after one printing and in small editions?

The new calendar year brought me few things to celebrate.

I had to move to a cheaper apartment that was in the southern part of Miramar. It was a small rectangle divided in half with a windowless bathroom. One entered through the side door of a building three or four stories high. Originally, the space had been part of the parking lot. Sometimes, especially at night when it was windy, bad smells blew in from the garbage dump. It was, without any doubt, the worst place I had ever lived.

I didn't have a steady job and could get up whenever I wanted. I had persuaded a library to mount an exhibit of my paintings, so I worked there every afternoon until after midnight. I'd spend time with some friends who lived as I did. At night we'd hang out in the city. Once, chasing a rumor, we explored the streets of Río Piedras until we found a Middle Eastern restaurant near the mosque. There I ate dinner alone on countless nights, at a place that, at that hour, had very few customers, sitting next to Egyptian, Lebanese, and Palestinian import merchants, watching lengthy musical shows, in which, almost always, a woman sang and danced in front of an impressive band. It was my way of retaining the taste of the world in my mouth. It was, also, a way of grieving.

Only on rare occasions would I get out of San Juan, because neither my car nor my friends' cars were in any shape to handle major expeditions. I became familiar with a poverty that was both human and material, similar to the one I had endured for years in foreign countries. But this poverty felt crueler for being in my own country. Here it was not embellished by exoticism, adventure or literature.

I was surrounded by a misery that people here always denied was comparable to the neighboring societies in the Caribbean and Latin America. My countrymen thus constructed a fortress with the mortar of our power lines, highways, shopping centers, colonialism, and the dollar. Our reasoning was false and limiting, confined to a belief that among us there were no barefoot children, that, like some species offensive to our eyes and good consciences, they had vanished when the country was opened to transnational companies and to an orgy of cement. We couldn't or shouldn't ask for more, which would seem senseless and ungrateful. But, despite appearances, air conditioners, refrigerators, the first personal computers, the country remained in the place it had occupied for hundreds of years. It preserved intact its handicaps, its persistent vocation as a disposable island, its beggarly gloating. Culture, aside from claustrophobic and belligerent ghettos, was always elsewhere. We kept repeating ourselves for almost five hundred years. We knew only how to admire or to scorn other countries that, basically, we didn't even know. We always preferred to see, not the truth, but an image we had created of them and of ourselves. It was a dreadful vicious circle.

I worked for short periods on community projects in towns adjacent to San Juan. I translated instruction manuals for cement mixers, lawn mowers, and electronic toys. I sought work as a journalist, in government offices, and in a greeting-card factory. I never stopped reading and thinking and thus produced my first books and art shows. One day, unexpectedly, I got a call from the university.

University teaching allowed me to move from Miramar and to buy a stereo set, a television, and a DVD player. I could now look forward to the weekend, knowing that I could escape by watching some film on the foreign movie channel. With my first paychecks, I could acquire the appliances that were already in countless homes, but which, for me, constituted a kind of life preserver.

I spent very little. My only luxuries were books and art materials. I got used to living as an introvert. San Juan and the country could, at the slightest provocation, inspire frustration and anger, but I tried not to fall back on those props. When all was said and done I accepted the life I was leading, whether out of heroism or resignation I don't know.

At the beginning of my second year as professor, I entered a classroom and discovered, at the back, sitting in the last seat in a row, someone I was sure I had met before. I looked at those paying attention to me from their desks and stopped at that face which I finally managed to place. He was the boy who, years earlier, had sought me out, shouting on a street in old San Juan. I remembered his first name but couldn't recall his last name. He had filled out and no longer had the freshness of youth. When the hour was over, I greeted him warmly. Vanity led me to assume he had read my name on the list of professors and had leapt at the chance to take one of my courses. I soon discovered that this was not the case, and that the surprise of spotting each other in the lecture hall had been mutual. He had to take the course because it was required for graduation. Otherwise, it held no interest for him at all. He had been at the university for five years and was anxious to finish his degree in French. We took leave of each other with chilly civility and for several classes I watched him come in late and leave early. He sat at the same desk he occupied the first day, took very few notes, did not participate in class, and often did not even deign to look at me. One morning, before class, I found him smoking on the second-floor balcony. I had no reason to avoid him and so I came over to say hello.

"One doesn't say *en base de* but rather *a base de* for 'on the basis of,'" he said.

It took a few seconds for me to realize that he was correcting something I said in class.

"It's an Anglicism," he added.

"You're right. Those are things one says without thinking," I said justifying myself, confused by the tone of our exchange.

"Do you like doing this?" he asked at the same time he made a sweeping gesture toward the corridors, the lecture rooms, the entire building.

I said yes, but I knew he wasn't convinced.

"The classics," I said, "were never what I thought I'd teach, but one can do a lot with them."

"But here?"

"Of course. Where else? I have no other place."

"You think they understand you, or care?"

"The students merely reflect the society. Perhaps the university can be an antidote for some of them."

He didn't speak any further and put out his cigarette. It was time to enter the classroom. The conversation had gone badly. I could understand him, however. I was sure that, if I were in his shoes, I would have a similar doom-and-gloom attitude. This explained his choice of seat in the room, his aggrieved silence and antipathy toward me. I knew that, in all probability, he was the best student I had, and I wanted to offer him the benefit of my goodwill.

As the weeks passed, we met several times before and after class. Our conversations lasted the time it took to smoke a cigarette. Thus I had news of his friend Guillermo, who had left to work in New York and was applying to graphic design institutes. I also found out that Alejandro had helped organize a poetry reading in a bar in San Juan and had smoked so much that night that he had spent the weekend with tachycardia. He didn't offer to show me his poems. It wasn't even clear to me that he had read them in public.

The first exam he took in the class was excellent, but in the next one he didn't get the highest grade. When he got it back, after having missed several classes, he came to see me.

"I don't care about the grade, but I'd like to know what's going on here."

I took the pages and explained each of the comments I had written in the margins. My status as professor created a barrier between us. I knew that my explanations didn't satisfy him, not because they weren't valid, but because this was not what bothered him. Alejandro couldn't get close without being aggressive. He'd compare himself to others and always arrive at arrogant conclusions. He thought he belonged in my place. I grew tired of his attitude and left him to his world.

I'd see him now and then on campus. He liked to sit on the benches around the humanities building, under the immense trees, to read, smoke, and drink coffee. Sometimes I saw him accompanied by a thin girl wearing glasses who built around herself a kind of impenetrable wall. They resembled one another, both of them taking on the same world-weary misery as if they were wearing hair shirts. On one occasion when I saw them together, we exchanged glances, but I knew, without a doubt, that I should not approach. They didn't seem to be a couple, but, on the other hand, they encompassed an exclusive and despotic territory.

I knew our country and could imagine the causes of their isolation. The hard, unfriendly façade that they flaunted was only a feeble, and, in the long run, ineffectual defense of their pride. Alejandro and his friend, and others like them, lived in a society that barely accommodated them. They'd meet in the hallways, plazas, and classrooms of the university, after spending years as pariahs. Some literature, language, or art professor would take them under his wing and raise the flimsy bastions of their vocations as writers or artists. Behind them remained the dark, conflictive past that had brought them this far, the history of an outcast's failure to adapt, which would probably never be resolved.

And so, despite everything, I offered him my friendship. One day I invited him home, adding that if he wanted to, he could bring his friend. He looked surprised, as if the second part of my proposal had caught him off guard, but he ended up accepting, unable to completely hide his eagerness.

They arrived almost two hours late. Knowing our local bad habit of not writing down addresses I went out on my balcony several times to see if I could see them looking for the house.

Giving a false excuse, Alejandro and the girl, whose name was Rosa, finally came up to the top floor where I had moved and sat down on the uncomfortable sofa that I had bought from the landlord and which was right next to my workshop. This space would attract the attention of visitors because of my paintings, either finished or in process, leaning on top of one another against the wall, and the little piles of metal and wood I'd bring in from the street to make assemblages. I presumed, as I took curiosity for granted, that at some moment they would show some interest in my work. There was not one mention, however, during the whole night: it was as if my work were invisible.

I measured the magnitude of our misery. We dug trenches and fired weapons, as having received so many blows it was impossible not to expect more of the same. Thus we had to suffer this idiotic chitchat and drink beers in order to access some simulacrum of friendly exchange.

On a table in front of the sofa stood a pile of poetry books. The girl picked up one and opened it at random, pausing barely a few seconds on some line or stanza.

"I wonder how they can find anyone to publish this," she said, grimacing at Alejandro.

The discarded volume was by Paul Celan. I decided it was pointless to mention who he was.

Alejandro glanced through an anthology of French poetry.

"Can I borrow this?" he asked.

I went to get us something to drink, figuring this would be the last time I would see the book. I heard them whispering. My absence had made them talkative. I had been stupid to invite them. I put on a record to make the night bearable for myself.

"Who's that?" Alejandro asked, after sipping from the can of beer.

"You don't know Léo Ferré?"

"No."

"He's a great singer. He put Rimbaud and Apollinaire to music, and his own lyrics are also very good. He died recently, last July 14. He was an anarchist. You should listen to his songs."

"He really put Apollinaire to music?"

"Yes, and other poets. He has an album dedicated to Aragon."

"Can I hear them?"

"What?"

"Apollinaire's poems."

"I don't think I have them."

Finally I saw him show some interest in something and come out of his shell a bit. I went to look in the pile of cassettes from my time in Paris, but I didn't find the tape.

"So, you like Apollinaire."

"Yes, a lot. The *Calligrammes* are marvelous. I took a class with Marta and they were the best thing we read. The rest, Breton, Desnos, Char, and the surrealists who came later all seemed too cerebral. But Apollinaire is something else."

I didn't tell him that Apollinaire wasn't exactly a surrealist. Marta must have been Marta Gómez Centeno, a French professor, with a PhD from Paris, and many years at the university. I had heard that she was good at giving language classes. She also knew how to inspire her students, and from generation to generation, they created circles of admirers around her. She taught more than the mere rigors of grammar and would show foreign films and organize gatherings and the visits of intellectuals. People gossiped that at her house, some years ago, with the help of a male photographer friend of hers, she had led sessions in "liberating the body" and among her refreshing new approaches were such Francophone goings-on as *ménages à trois*.

Aside from the gossip, Marta had been a pioneer, an initiator bringing into the country such diverse currents as structuralism, anti-phallocentrism, the first movies by Almodóvar and erotic comics. For years she had had a major impact on the lives of many students. Independent of what one thought of her methods, or of her, this was no small achievement. I had never met her but I knew that, if I had stayed in the country like Alejandro and Rosa, I would have been a member of her group. Recently she had surprised everyone with the publication of some slim volumes of poetry and narrative. She had created a big stir with her use of language (which, from what I heard, reproduced the most exact nuances of colloquial speech) and with handling subjects rarely touched upon, so to speak, in the country. Speculating on the bisexuality of Muñoz Marín, with abundant psychoanalytical, semiotic, or postmodern references in accessible language, she was taking a risk but also, as far as I could see, an opportunistic path to fame. Someone had written unjustly, in bad faith, that she was a female version of the gay artist Antonio Martorell. Her work was suspiciously didactic, useful because of this very fact for consumption by young, impressionable readers. She was that kind of egocentric island artist, aspiring to gather crumbs of recognition in a society almost totally lacking in artistic criteria and culture. She was a kind of simplistic native translator of modernity and postmodernity, at those inevitable key moments in which the official culture (aside from its folkloric traditions) needed to look good. She and a few others were perfect for rousing speeches, posters, and the front rows of inaugurations and funerals. They had opted, in detriment to their talent, to be court jesters in a court that wasn't even sure if it existed.

"Did you see Marta's last article in *Diálogo*?"

"Rosa hates men," Alejandro explained. I had read the article in the university newspaper. It was an ambiguous and ironic homage to the woman who had tried to kill Andy Warhol and in it, in a muddled way, she connected the woman's will to kill with the generic use of the masculine gender in Spanish.

"She's right," said Rosa. "Why not say *las hombres*?"

"Don't start with that again, you always end up saying dumb things."

"They might sound dumb to you, but we have to start somewhere. Why not call you *la hombre*?"

"Marta was goofing around."

"Well, I'm not. And Marta wasn't goofing around either. She was very serious."

The conversation was all about people I didn't know. They talked about classmates and professors whom they'd nicknamed the title of a book or the name of an author.

"Derridito didn't want to give me an incomplete." I was irritated by Rosa's habit of not including me in the conversation, refusing to acknowledge my presence, as if she needed to be hostile.

"What were you going to write about?" I asked to force her to look at me.

"The contemporary short story in the Caribbean. Or rather women short-story writers in Cuba and Puerto Rico, but this was too inclusive, so I ended up limiting it to Puerto Rico."

I imagined the content of her paper. The women writers would be Marta Gómez Centeno and two or three of her contemporaries, whom Rosa probably knew personally. It was a legitimate topic, but at the same time a testimony to the limitations of her knowledge and curiosity. Derridito probably realized this and refused to validate her laziness and narrow perspective.

The evening progressed with difficulty. It was one more in a long chain of attempts to create bonds among people who supposedly had a lot to say to each other. Throughout the years I met many like Alejandro and Rosa. Folks who remained stuck, fixated on their defenses, too sick to be able to engage in a conversation in which they weren't mouthpieces of some cause or, what was almost the same thing, of some retaliation.

We Puerto Ricans were eloquent and friendly when we needed to unburden ourselves. When we couldn't stand it any longer, we'd ask people to listen to us speak empty words, without pointing out the causes of our own misery, for which we didn't want to be responsible. We loved monologues, and yet our loneliness terrified us.

As we said good-bye, I realized that Alejandro hadn't wanted the night to go that way. His gesture was almost imperceptible, but firm and eloquent. Perhaps he just couldn't do any better. But it was not my job to save him. Bidding him good night, I knew that he would return to being just another student. I would teach him in class, correct his exams, but his life would remain distant from mine.

I spoke to him only once more before the end of the semester. I ran into him across from the humanities building and asked him for a cigarette. "Buy your own" was his terse reply.

2

I had no news of him for years. I was able, with friends, and
later with a couple of girlfriends, to take a few trips. I returned
to Paris on several occasions and only bothered to visit the Pétrements and Simone and her father. I took a photo of myself
under the street sign of the Astrolabe cul-de-sac and entered
the building where I had lived. Beside the entrance door I
paused, attentive and silently, musing on how everything,
basically, vanished without leaving a trace. I traveled to other
countries and on my last trip I didn't even consider going to
France. My life was in San Juan, and I knew that Europe was
a chapter to which I would not return. There, in a few years, I
had lived with an intensity that was hard to match in the life
that would follow. I would accept the deficiencies that surrounded me: even though I didn't want to admit it, I no longer experienced my commitments and passions in the same
way. I would write, paint, or sculpt, knowing that nobody
was awaiting my creations, that it would be difficult for me
to publish or exhibit my work, and even harder for anyone to
read, see, or appreciate what I offered. I knew these difficulties
were not exclusive to my country, and that even in great cities,
though probably for other reasons, they were the norm. But
those places elsewhere, even though they didn't shower success on some, were more enjoyable. I'd look at art magazines
or the latest book reviews and couldn't help recognizing that
the world didn't offer everyone equal opportunities.

I acquired, in those years outside Puerto Rico, the habit
and the pleasure of walking. Even in San Juan, where uncon-
trollable growth limited the intimate joy of strolling, I went

everywhere on foot. Hundreds of times I walked along tree-less avenues, where the thirst for profit and makeshift expansion had destroyed all beauty. Frequently I imagined being far away, walking along different streets than these. Thus, in my fantasy life, I crossed deserts, continents, and cities on foot: the eastern Mediterranean, Egypt, the plateaus of Tibet, Patagonia. The voyage would begin in books and unfailingly run into the dirty sidewalks of San Juan, the only place in the world where I could dream of distant lands and cities. Without intending to, I became part of the landscape, and there were many people who would recognize me because they had seen me during the hours of my walk.

One Sunday morning during Christmas vacation, I was taking a walk in the direction of Old San Juan with the woman who would become my wife. She pointed out a car that had stopped and someone who was calling to me. Approaching, I saw a fat woman and a girl in the passenger seat. I didn't know either of them, but I heard a familiar voice. I bent down to discover that the driver was none other than Alejandro Espinal. He had turned into a husky man and he smiled to greet me. While the traffic avoided his car, which was blocking the road, he told me he was visiting and would like to see me. After the woman who I presumed was his sister wrote down my telephone number, they immediately took off. As Alejandro had vanished from my memory so completely, I felt surprised by his interest.

In the following days he called me several times. I was about to move once again, and on two or three occasions I had to postpone our date. Each time he answered the phone he told me something about his life. Thus I learned, before seeing him, that he was studying for a PhD in French in a North American university, that he had spent a year in France on an exchange program, and that, even though ultimately he had not been able to throw himself entirely into his work, he was a poet.

The news, the tone of the conversation, and his desire to tell me who he had become, augured healthy changes. I assumed it would be possible to have a conversation. I left the early hours of an afternoon open so that he could come get me to go for lunch.

He didn't get out to come greet my partner or to see our son. He honked the horn until I came down to the street. Immediately I realized something wasn't right. His frantic way of smoking and driving and his convoluted ways of expressing himself portended an ill-fated encounter. He didn't have the courtesy to take into account my preferences, but rather, after driving around, revealing how little he knew the city, he stopped in front of a Puerto Rican restaurant in ramshackle Villa Palmeras. It was the place least likely to please me because I hadn't eaten meat for years. I had to settle for plantain fritters and a glass of water. We sat at the only free table, beside a cage of hens and near another filled with rabbits. Alejandro ordered a beer and some dish he wouldn't be able to find in the restaurants around his university. He ate, drank, and smoked all at once. Annoyed, I was forced to listen to his story.

It had taken him more time than it should have to graduate college. Despite setbacks, he had been a good student, and the French department at the University of Chicago had given him a fellowship. He had been there for a year and then spent the following year in France. The French university required of the foreign students that they teach a few hours of classes in their own language. As Alejandro was studying in an American university, they had taken for granted that he spoke English. His English was acceptable, but he didn't feel comfortable enough to teach it. I already knew that Alejandro was difficult, tending to get entangled in impossible situations. He had put the department chair, his students, and himself through an infernal semester, repeating tirelessly that he was willing to teach everything they wanted in Spanish but not

English. The situation contributed to the fact that many students avoided him. He felt abandoned, barred from being able to make new friends. The longed-for city, which he had finally reached, turned into a stage upon which he meandered with his loneliness. For a while he'd spend the whole day reading in parks or going to movie theaters and bookstores, taking refuge every two or three hours in some café.

One Sunday night—Paris would make it harder to be alone on Sundays—he pulled up to a bar. His neighbor offered him a cigarette. This was an unexpected event in a society where strangers didn't speak to each other. The brand of cigarette and the man's accent were British. This began the story of a fleeting and ultimately one-sided love affair Alejandro related to me, in fragments. Thus I learned that he was homosexual. Now what I knew about him was much more understandable.

He fell in love with Kenneth Phillpott, an art history student whose father was English and mother was Swiss. The main point in this story seemed to be how attracted he was to his beauty, but also in equal or larger measure to the seductive power of his wealth. The relationship distanced him from the classrooms and dormitory in the university district. With his lover he got to know the Paris of the French, infinitely more appealing than the hangouts of his classmates. His contact with real citizens filled him with pride and he was willing to sacrifice his fellowship year. Before he met the Englishman, his relationships had been tussles with classmates and a secret union with a priest at the high school where he had studied. This had been the reason for his transfer to a public school as the scandal had forced him to leave.

For Phillpott, Alejandro didn't seem to be much more than a seasonal conquest. His sense of privilege made him careless and unpredictable. He could live, if he wished, in three or four countries where he had friends and owned houses. He could spend the summer in Capri just as he could in Rhodes or on the Costa Brava. He didn't suffer the personal, social, and monetary constraints of his lover. For Alejandro, Kenneth was the passport to his desires. With him he could stay in Europe and gain access to the life of his dreams.

The relationship had its setbacks. Kenneth left him in Paris, which, in the long run, had certain advantages, since Alejandro returned to the university and survived the final exams. But Kenneth's trip to London lasted longer than he had promised, and Paris was not the same without the Englishman's presence. He had to leave his room at the Cité Universitaire and take a room at a hotel on Rue Mabillon. Kenneth had not offered him his apartment. He waited for him for a month. Their time together was emotional and brief, because at the end of August Phillpott left for the Balearics and Alejandro had to return to his university in the United States. There had been no further invitation on the part of the Englishman, but instead Alejandro became aware of Kenneth's long daily conversations with some unknown man, out of reach of Alejandro's hearing.

The day they said good-bye, Alejandro took a walk along the poplar groves of the Tuileries and responded to an Arab who called him over. He made love without exchanging a word, like a voiceless body. The next day he returned but didn't find the Arab. He offered himself to another who went off with his wallet. Forty-eight hours later he flew to Illinois without a cent and with a venereal disease.

From the first days of the semester, he knew he wouldn't be able to make it to the end. He couldn't progress with the readings because he'd become obsessed with some detail and read over and over again endlessly. In the end, he was called into the director's office and had to transfer to another university. In January, he entered the new program as an interim student and remained there, for better or for worse, almost three years. He needed one more course to finish. I asked what he thought he'd do the thesis on, and after a lot of talk, I still didn't have a clear idea of what his focus would be. He talked in circles, losing the thread, leaving any idea or plan half-baked, always as if with an urgent need to change direction.

The waiter took away our plates. On his, the food was mixed together and picked at, as if a child had been playing with it to amuse himself. He ordered two desserts and two coffees one after the other. He lit a cigarette without noticing that one was smoking in the ashtray.

Lunch had lasted too long. I kept him from ordering a third coffee, using the excuse that I had to take care of a problem with the move. Fighting with the traffic in a useless expense of energy, he drove me home. He would be leaving in two or three days and I didn't ask for his address or press him to come see me again. I shook his hand without knowing what to say.

For a few days he remained in my thoughts. His was one of those tragic lives attracted to literature. I had come close to madness myself and knew that I could have ended up like Alejandro. A crisis, an error, or one more hopeless illusion would have been enough to send me to where he was. There was something in his insanity that I shared. I didn't know how to define it exactly, but a look in his eyes communicated a pain I had not seen elsewhere.

Around that time I distanced myself from books. For the first time in my life, I stopped reading novels and poetry. I would buy art books from catalogs—because they were practically impossible to obtain in Puerto Rico—and would devote my creative efforts to painting and sculpting. I even thought that the well of words had dried up. From time to time I'd pick out of my library some book I hadn't read, which was almost always a novel. I'd read about a fourth and always leave them unfinished, indifferent to their denouements. I often went to bookstores without even pausing in front of the shelves of literature. I didn't keep up with the new writers coming out and for the first time I had to ask others who was this or that author and what was important about them. I even reached the point of getting annoyed at the reputations of others, perhaps because I couldn't admit to myself the suspicion that my energy and willpower had been, in the long run, insufficient.

I spent months working with wood, immersed in a rhythm of gouges, mallets, and axes, in which there was no place for words and adjectives. It was liberating. I worked with my hands, with the earthy and tangible. Little by little I was creating the world I would take to a museum in San Juan. I already had a date for the show and some money donated by a sponsor. I was enthralled with my tools, with their long tradition that enabled me to do without electrical machinery. I cut and polished by hand, awash in the poetry of sweat and muscle. My books remained in the past, buried in the warehouses of their incompetent publishers. I didn't present myself to anyone as a writer and was annoyed by my wife's habit to announce to people the lost existence of my books. I reached the point of preferring my body to my mind. The scars on my hands were a source of pride as were the conversations I carried on with carpenters and cabinetmakers in the lines buying wood from timber dealers.

A few days before the show opened, when I was already beginning to set it up, I answered the telephone. On the other end I heard a man's voice. Alejandro Espinal had returned. While I listened to him, I realized that it wasn't during vacation time but rather in the middle of the academic semester. I imagined that he might have finished his studies, but I realized that this was impossible. Since our last meeting, enough time hadn't passed. As on other occasions, his conversation over the phone was coherent and even pleasant. I again had hopes that he might be doing better. In some way, the nature of which

I didn't understand, I was drawn to Alejandro's life. Perhaps through him I was trying to confirm my own assumptions or to confront my doubts, to see up to what point I was similar or foreign to what he was. I couldn't see him right away, but I invited him to come by the museum the night of the opening.

I was taken up with a long list of tasks during those days. The night of the opening arrived and before anyone could enter, I went around the rooms. There was the alphabet of my vertebrate forms, of my bones of wood. All that remained of my literary past were a few words written in block letters on some of the paintings that hung on the walls. I stood still for a second and breathed with satisfaction. The silence washed over me and vibrated on my skin.

I received the public and, as occurs in these situations, enjoyed with numerous people conversations that almost always revolved around congratulations. The work was received enthusiastically, but that night there were no buyers. At some point I went out to the entrance hall looking for catalogs and saw that Alejandro was studying the piece that, under an arch, opened the way to the exhibit. I went to greet him. He had already gone around the rooms and had liked the exhibit very much. He elaborated some ideas that didn't seem relevant to me. Art wasn't literature.

At least he looked pretty well. He had gained weight and looked older. He said he had written some comments in the guest book and wanted to know what I thought of them. He added that he was writing and wanted me to read his texts. Someone came looking for me and I had to say good-bye.

Later I saw him smoking near the cocktail table in the beautiful patio inside the museum. When the night was over, I looked for him but he had gone.

The next day I left with my family for a beach house in the west. I relaxed a few days and didn't think about anything.

When we returned I found on the answering machine a couple of messages from journalists requiring an immediate response and six messages from Alejandro. In each he said the same thing: he wanted to see me, wanted to give me his poems. So much insistence eradicated my desire to call him. I didn't have to, anyway, as the next day he called again and I was the one who answered the phone.

He came to get me soon after and we went to dinner at a Middle Eastern restaurant. It was no longer the one in Río Piedras, which had closed. Now there were several places like this in the city with food that was quite delicious and belly dancing on Fridays and Saturdays.

He asked me if I had read what he had written in the guest book. I hadn't and promised that when I returned to the museum I would take the trouble to look at it. His persistence was exaggerated, but at that point I thought nothing of it. What caught my attention, however, was the difficulty he had in choosing what food to order. The waiter came back to the table several times and I was beginning to feel exasperated. Then he told me the story that astounded me.

Although he was still on leave, he had decided to abandon his studies. I was the first person to whom he was telling this. He only needed a couple of courses and the thesis to finish the PhD, but some months ago, when he was still an active student, he had thrown it all overboard. He had begun a relationship with a man, the son of Puerto Ricans, who worked as a janitor in the dormitories. At the beginning he hadn't gone beyond spying on him, getting to know his name, starting conversations with him. But he couldn't get him out of his head when he'd sit at a table in the library to read seventeenth-century French texts.

He would go to the showers, which were separated by cubicles, and would nearly reach the point of fainting from the big clouds of steam in his long baths. He would hang out there hoping that the man would show up with his cleaning cart. Finally he succeeded. His skin was all wrinkled by the dampness, when he heard the door open. He stepped out of the cubicle and presented himself to the janitor. With unexpected boldness, he opened his pants. They entered one of the showers, and Alejandro experienced a happiness he thought he had lost.

The next day he met with Miguel again, and they established a routine. He'd wait for him in his room, would suck him off or let him fuck him. His neighbors suspected the comings and goings, but for Alejandro the gossip was exciting. He had a man, a real man now, and he wanted to throw himself into his new identity, into the role he was playing in this drama. Melancholy had vanished. He barely went to class and read whatever he felt like reading: Camus, Montaigne, Boris Vian.

Sometimes he invited Miguel to lunch. Nights, though, did not belong to him. The janitor made it clear that he had a wife and children, and Alejandro agreed to keep their relationship secret.

One Saturday, Miguel came to his room with a boy he said was his cousin and they all went out for some beers. As night fell, they came back drunk to his room, and Miguel pressed him to suck both their penises. They both possessed him and Alejandro discovered the charms of being treated with indifference.

There were other meetings and Miguel asked him to shave his whole body. Alejandro was fucked in bathrooms and on car seats and more than once, almost publicly, at the entrance of the basement where the brooms, pails, and detergent were kept. One day, Miguel took him to a smoke-filled apartment, in which four men were arguing around a table full of bottles. In the next room, he was possessed by each one of them. At the end, he thought he didn't have to accept his share of the money.

He gave into Miguel. He put up with his whims, his increasingly bad treatment, and the men he brought him. He assumed his condition as prostitute, with some glimmers of sanity such as a big box of condoms on his night table. Towards the end of the semester, he dropped out of all his courses except one and invented an excuse not to come to San Juan to spend his vacation. He convinced himself that everything was going well, but something told him that he shouldn't see his parents. He stayed during New Year's week in the deserted dormitory. He had to concede that Miguel owed it to his family to spend the holiday with them. Perhaps the fruit of his exploitation had bought the toys or the Christmas dinner.

He'd spend time indefinitely in the showers. Loneliness, which had not abandoned him, was pernicious. He wrote poems, most of which he would give to me that night, in which I would discover his strange and clearly hermetic voice, which seemed not to have any relationship with his life, except for the spaces between words. He expressed a hard, dry, breathless, skinless eroticism full of references to a world that couldn't be transmitted but which remained in some form in his verse. He spoke without speaking and his texts were the image of an open mouth that forgot, on the very threshold of enunciation, how to scream.

He spent New Year's Eve on the street. On the days before it had snowed and with the low temperatures the poplar trees were covered with ice. He sat on a frozen bench and awaited the twelve strokes of the bell. He listened to the noisemakers and to the toasts. He knew, in that moment, that he was one of the most miserable beings on earth.

He didn't see Miguel again until the semester began. He noticed that Miguel kept him at a distance but he felt that, with patience, things would work out. He awaited him in the showers, looked for him in the hallways.

One day some man came to his room. He needed money. But Alejandro barely had any. He received the man's blow with resignation, as if he had always been waiting for it. He gave him a couple of bills and couldn't refuse to go with him. Beside the telephone booth, they waited for some guys to

come get them. In the front seat were two of the men he already knew. They went to where the other two were. On this
occasion they didn't retire to a room, but rather on the couch
or on the rug, they took turns fucking him while they watched
a football game. Finally, urged on by his clients, Miguel possessed him. He moved over him with cruelty, pulling him by
the hair, insulting him. Finally, humiliated, he remained on the
floor, shivering. He listened to the men's voices and clinking
glasses. He felt a hand on his chest and opened his eyes. He
thought it was Miguel getting close to him, repentant. Several
arms held him down. Miguel ordered him to keep quiet. He
felt then the incredibly hot stream of urine, the insults, and
belly laughs.

The next morning he applied for a sabbatical leave with the
pretext of illness in the family and a few days later was in his
sister's apartment in New York City. Perhaps he had wished
for this outcome, because running away had unexpectedly
emptied him of purpose. The reasons for it, however, were
kept a secret. He told his sister and the family another story.
    Almost right away he was lucky. An acquaintance that
worked in the Education Department gave Alejandro a job,
midsemester, as a substitute teacher. He traveled every day to
a school in the Bronx to deal with kids who gladly received
the news that their teachers were absent. I found this difficult
to believe, as I couldn't imagine him working with students
at an elementary level, but apparently he worked responsibly
and with enthusiasm, even with success. With the first checks,
he could afford a tiny room on Eighth Avenue. He'd spend
his free time in the city, browsing in bookstores, reading and
writing in the cafés of the Village. He came to feel that he had
a satisfactory, even a rich life.
    One day, in the Librairie de France in Rockefeller Center,

he met a Frenchman. They went to have dinner, to a movie, and to a gay bar. That night he slept in his apartment. They got to know each other well, and Alejandro went on to form part of an international social group attracted by the aura of New York City. Swedes and Hungarians, Maghrebis and Brits, a Japanese lesbian, a German athlete who dyed his hair and was over sixty, formed part of this sophisticated, frivolous, and diffuse conclave.

Serge and his friends offered him what in former times Kenneth Phillpott had given him a glimpse of: an amusing and decadent world in which books and artists, love affairs, and scandals were common currency. There was always something to do: a party, a movie, excellent marijuana. They had fun going to exotic restaurants (How was the Mongolian food? When should we have a Paul Bowles night?); in bars, cafes, and discotheques, they savored the lustful eye candy of an endless flow of pectorals, crotches, and butts. Most of the group came from rich white societies, and perhaps because of that, they were attracted to the most extreme forms of otherness. Latinos, Blacks, and Asians, especially those who came from very poor and violent conditions, were the objects of desire they fought over and manipulated. Alejandro could suspect that his origins had something to do with Serge's interest and the friendship of his circle, but he soon realized that they coveted neither his body nor his personality. They were seeking a noble savage to play at being barbarians.

Alejandro didn't earn enough to keep up with this lifestyle. Serge grew tired of him and didn't hide that he was after a Haitian whose genitals were legendary. The distancing between them gradually closed him off from the group. Only Peter, the older German guy skilled in physical culture, continued to call and ask him out to dinner. In this relationship the roles of father and lover were mixed together. Together they went to doctors' appointments, gyms, and concerts. He had a key

to Peter's apartment and for the first time in his life he didn't
have to worry about the cost of things. He should have noticed, however, that his only peaceful relationship had been
with an impotent man.

After some months, Peter traveled to Germany to attend
the reading of a will. The separation, which was supposed to
last just a few days, was inexplicably prolonged. Alejandro received calls, letters, and gifts, and finally, an envelope with a
stranger's handwriting. One of Peter's sisters was writing to
inform him that he had been found dead. It turns out that
Peter had cancer, and so, it had probably been just as well
that his heart stopped. The German hadn't told him anything
about his health problems. That silence, which perhaps would
have been temporary, was more devastating than his death.

He did the best he could to live normally. He went to work
but he felt absent. One day he didn't get up to take the train.
He spent days in his apartment without getting out of bed,
playing with the idea of dying. His sister took him to the psychiatric hospital, after getting worried about his staying home
and finding out, when she went to visit him, that he had torn
his books to shreds and destroyed the bathroom mirror.

He spent the first days sleeping. He sensed that men were
coming over to him and asking questions. Later, therapy began
and life with the other patients. He'd see the psychiatrist in the
mornings and spend the rest of the day smoking and reading
detective novels. He was a model patient, calm and coopera-
tive; soon the doctors released him, giving his place to a doubtlessly more colorful patient. He shared an apartment with his
sister and gradually returned to his routine of streets, parks,
and cafeterias. Wherever he sat he composed new texts. This
work made him think of returning to Puerto Rico. I asked him
why and he said something that was both obvious and terrible:
he was looking for someone who could read what he wrote.

One morning he got on a plane. He brought with him only
one suitcase with clothes, papers, and a few books. He had

the conviction that he should move back to Puerto Rico. At first he would live with his parents. Amazingly, he still had my phone number and Enrique Esteves's. He called both of us right away. The night we talked took place two weeks after he had arrived. As the hours passed he told me this story, first in the restaurant and then sitting on the deserted steps of the monument to Baldorioty, facing the El Condado lagoon. He had already seen Esteves several times by then.

I was moved by his tale. I didn't know how to help him, although I thought of a few friends who might be willing to mobilize their influence. At the very least, I could offer him some company. It would do him good to go out from time to time.

Later that night, when I dropped him off at his house, he asked me to wait a minute. He came out immediately with a large envelope. In it was a group of poems. He said he would call me to see what I thought. I shook his hand looking at him straight in the eye, as if trying to transmit the certainty that I had listened to and heard him.

Before I took off he detained me. "I would like to introduce you to Enrique Esteves."

"I've seen him around. He teaches at the university."

"He was my professor and he lived in Paris in the early sixties, when almost nobody was doing that."

"That's more or less how he has always been."

"It's true. Anyway I think you both would be interested in knowing each other."

"Make a date, and let me know."

"Okay, good-bye."

"Don't let things get you down, now."

He knew that my words were a mere gesture.

"Please, read the poems."

I didn't take into account his insistence. I was given unpublished texts to read all the time. I knew there would be further unpleasant surprises and meetings, after which the friendship probably would not survive. As Alejandro was tremendously vulnerable, I'd read the material not as quickly as was desired, and, if possible, give the most positive critique I could. I would do this when I had some spare time and felt like it.

The next day he called for the first time. Fortunately I wasn't the one who answered and I didn't have to deal with the matter. But when in the following days he left perhaps a dozen messages on the answering machine, I decided to go to my workshop and open the envelope.

Many of the poems were more than a page long. They were difficult, had no narrative, and, as I've said, suggested rather than expressed an unfulfilled love relationship, without any resolution. The poet—and without any doubt Alejandro was a poet—masked himself with references to a vast literary tradition. When I read him I had the impression I was going to a strange place where I would never arrive. But the voyage was without a doubt worth the trouble.

In a pizzeria in El Condado I expressed my enthusiasm. Surprisingly, Alejandro received it with indifference, obsessing over secondary aspects that my comments didn't deal with and about which he wanted feedback. The doggedness was on the point of driving me bats. I didn't know what he wanted. I didn't know what more to say to him. I didn't understand the purpose of his cryptic questions. I realized that for him the poems had turned into something more than literary texts. It was as if they were a body that had to be acknowledged with undivided attention. He was a child who was demanding all the love in the world.

He had left a piece of pizza half finished; he was playing with the drops of humidity that had accumulated on the bottle of beer, and gazing away at some indeterminate point, he was looking for something I hadn't said. My reading had turned out to be a failure. It wasn't enough for him, because nothing could fill the need to hear something he couldn't even define or identify. That black hole swallowed everything for him.

That night I brought him a signed copy of my last book. I never knew if he read it or simply glanced through a few pages. It contained a short novel and several stories that were about the European experience. I assumed he would be interested and have something to tell me. When I saw him again, he made only a vague comment and asked me if I knew Steven Armstrong. I had come across the name in bookstores but had never read him. According to him, Armstrong he had followed a trajectory similar to mine and we both shared a deliberate simplicity. He offered to loan me the only book he had of his, a compilation of reviews and miscellaneous texts. A couple of days later, I found it in the mailbox of my house. The title was extraordinary: *The Usefulness of Blindness.*

I couldn't imagine what finding this book would mean for me, or, likewise, the magnitude of Alejandro's intuition in recommending that I read it. I gathered most of the texts Armstrong had published in literary magazines before his success, during a black period of need and struggle. They were mostly book reviews, which the brilliance of his writing had turned into real essays. Amazingly, he reviewed a few years before I discovered them many of the authors and books that had influenced me. He had lived in France and, upon returning to New York, had thrown himself into writing about his French affinities and influences.

He dedicated two works to Neptune, one to his great novel and another, written on the occasion of his death, to the significance of his literary life. I could have written them. However, what left me thunderstruck was the story of his discovery of Pierre Plon, who at that time was almost unknown. He had found, on the table of a bookstore in Saint-Germain-des-Prés, the chronicle of his expeditions to the jungle. Armstrong had nothing to do with this world. He was not an anthropologist, archeologist, historian, or Latin Americanist, and yet some mysterious impulse made him acquire the book and read it from beginning to end in two and a half days. He was fascinated by the perspective of the man who became the raconteur of a millennial culture at the very moment of its annihilation. Without any logic whatsoever, since he didn't have a publisher, nor was this his line of work, he decided immediately to translate it. The task took him over two years. During that time he exchanged several letters with the author and took a trip to Paris expressly to get to know him. When he arrived, he met with the news that Plon had just died, run over on the Boulevard Raspail. Toward the end of his text, the writer dedicated a few paragraphs to a melancholy conversation with a friend of Plon's, in a Parisian apartment filled with books and Asian objects. In the last lines he provided his name. It was Didier Pétrement.

Aside from these pieces, Armstrong had written others on Antonin Artaud, César Vallejo, Knut Hamsen, Paul Celan, Kafka, the early Milan Kundera, on the Lisbon of Pessoa and the Paris of Walter Benjamin. These, together with introductions to French poets and a note on Roberto Juarroz, took me back again to the part of me that had tried to put time into words. I realized writing was not dead for me, but rather, under a surface of detachment and pretended indifference, I still had the urge.

Armstrong's book reconnected me with the endeavor of writing, eventually influencing my way of living. It took me over a year to return to making a text, but during that period *The Usefulness of Blindness* was there reminding me that reading and writing were useless yet unavoidable, that it was the same in Paris or in San Juan: this was my way of occupying time and space.

3

I would see Alejandro often. Every week he'd call me several
times and it would seem to me that on the telephone was
where his thinking was most coherent, as if direct human presence stimulated him too much or pulled him, simultaneously,
in two or more different directions. He always wanted to get
together, to bring me new poems or consult me on some, often slight, matter regarding his search for work. It was obvious
that he was still in bad shape and could not solve his problems
on his own. More than once I urged him to seek help, but my
advice didn't help much, since, in any event, he couldn't pay
for therapy.

We'd go out to eat and afterwards take a stroll. It wasn't
always pleasant to be with him, to witness the unstoppable
wheel of his hang-ups. With our walks I sought to lighten the
topics of our conversations and to find a way, at the very least,
to enjoy myself. I was showing him a city he had never seen.
Alejandro was, like so many citizens of San Juan, a stranger to
the space in which he lived. He had always gone around the
city by car, blinded by speed.

On the walls of the old city I knew where there was a staircase that went down to the breakwater. There, along a narrow path, one could go around the Morro fortress and gaze
at the wide expanse of the bay. One could see the city and on
the other shore Cataño, and far away, on the hills, the faint
vibration of the lights which must be in Guaynabo or in Ba-
yamón. We'd go around the edges of the fort until we reached
the walls of the cemetery, where we'd climb up to a little pile
of stones among which lay the broken pieces of marble from

ancient gravestones. There we'd sit to watch the sea, which had a mysterious beauty especially on moonless nights. The dark water felt then, more than other times, like the desert that separated us from the world.

Turning his back on the dead, whose tombs we'd see from where we sat on top of the wall, Alejandro would seem calm, maybe, for a moment, feeling better. When we'd go back, I would lead him along the least-trafficked streets until we got to the windows—almost always opened—of a bookbinder's shop. We'd peer into the dim interior piled with books, the tables covered with tools, presses, and sheets of paper. I'd take him to certain street corners and point so that he would look at the ground. Near his feet were small sewer drains, polished smooth by shoes and the elements, with dates from a century ago. Other times we'd visit the decayed beauty of Santurce or the side streets of Alto del Cabro, listening to the chickens and pigs that lived together in tiny lots with their owners. Río Piedras was a dark sector at night and, awaiting the garbage trucks, an olfactory adventure. In the Plaza de la Convalecencia, next to the church was an ice-cream parlor run by Chinese that remained open late. We'd have an ice cream or a milkshake, sitting on a bench under the stars of the tropics. We'd talk about Armstrong's book: we thought a lot about it and wanted to write about him. Alejandro would ask me about my times in Paris but would get impatient with my stories, regretting that he had asked. He was incapable of listening. Dealing with him meant putting up with this tyranny. I believe there was never an occasion when he didn't talk about his poems or repeat a part of his own history.

One day he took me to Esteves's house. I had seen him go by almost invisibly along the hallways of the humanities building. He was small and delicate, perpetually silent. I knew very little about him. Nothing prepared me for meeting him.

We parked in Río Piedras and went to a three-story building. We climbed to the third floor by a narrow staircase; on the first landing was a strong smell of urine. We knocked and listened a moment after a successive unlocking of several locks. Under the doorframe Esteves appeared, and, behind him, we noticed an extraordinary disorder. After our hellos, we went into the living room that faced onto a small balcony upon which there were many pots with dead plants. Esteves moved books, piles of papers, and a couple of plates with the leftovers of food so that we could sit on a sofa with broken springs into which I sank. On the coffee table there was an overflowing ashtray. Esteves offered coffee and Soberano brandy. We let the hot liquid rest, putting the cups wherever we could. We watched as he poured, blinded by a cigarette between his lips, into the coffee a long stream of amber-colored liquor, whose resinous fragrance brought back distant memories.

At the beginning, he made an effort not to look at me, but, strangely, I did not feel ignored. I observed that on the walls were two collages by El Boquio Alberty. I stood up to look at them, turning my back on him. When I turned around, I found him looking at me.

"They're Boquios?" I asked, knowing the answer.

"You know him."

"Not personally, but I've seen whatever I've been able to, of his work."

"He was my friend. You must have seen that they are dedicated."

"They are good pieces."

"Like many that he did. Like many that were lost who knows where. I don't know if you know that he even sketched, for lack of materials, but also by design, with cigarette ash."

"So I have heard," I said taking the first sip of the strong and very bitter coffee, probably burnt.

"He's an artist," said Alejandro.

"Really? Please don't be offended if I don't know you. I've

been out of it for many years. I am sure that, if you had the eye and the curiosity to identify Roberto Alberty's, your work must have value. But I am no longer interested in painting. Besides, I don't see well and it's a big effort for me to go to galleries. I don't drive."

He drank from his cup and crushed the butt.

"Look, I want to show you something."

He left us alone. I saw in a mirror that he was looking for something under the bed. On top of the mahogany chest of drawers, there was a bottle of eucalyptus rubbing alcohol and talcum powder. He returned with a wooden frame, dusting off the glass with his hand. When he handed it to me, I couldn't believe what I was seeing. It was a small engraving by Matta. He was reelaborating his famous image of *The Poet*: a body with the head of an insect or bull, pointing a pistol—in whose barrel there's a lock—at the spectator. The paper was stained with damp spots. On the lower left edge there was a dedication to Esteves by Matta.

I raised my eyes. Esteves lit a cigarette and explained: "He gave it to me in '62. Around that time, in Paris, I once went by La Promenade de Venus café. This was where Breton, following the custom of heroic eras, gathered towards the end his few insignificant 'soldiers' who remained. I wanted to join his army of acolytes like the good provincial who enters history thirty years too late. Unfortunately I was rejected for being conservative, even if in that era, the 'Pope' was being abandoned by most and was willing to allow on his red carpet even the dumbest of the dumb. I didn't meet Matta there. I hadn't spoken to Breton for a long time. Benjamin Escarano, the Mexican poet, an excellent inventor of verbal machines, who died very young, introduced him to me in the café I went to regularly. We'd meet there often and spend a good hour talking. One day he came from his atelier with a roll of proofs of watercolors. He took one of the prints and asked for a pencil to sign it for me. But this was a long time ago. Anyway, I thought you'd be interested. I have other things that I'm sure you'd like to see, but I have to look for them. Come another day with more time if you wish and I'll show them to you."

That evening, which soon turned into night, Esteves completely won me over. He listened to Alejandro's poems with an openness and concentration that were commendable. What he said was pertinent and generous, without any pretention. We left late, and even had to go out to get another bottle of Soberano and something to eat. I observed his trembling hands, his discomfort in the armchair, his impressive tolerance for drink, and his indifference to his coughing attacks, which didn't prevent him from continuing to smoke, and I thought that the old poet spoke to us from an inaccessible and fearful place. When I said good night, I knew that I would be back.

Thus began our friendship. It wouldn't last long, just a few months. I soon learned that he was, predictably, very ill. Nevertheless, the cancer in his bones was a secret he didn't reveal until the end. His doctor gave him his dire prognosis and Esteves didn't visit him again, or any other doctor. He did nothing to vary his way of life. He still attended, while the pains didn't paralyze him, his classes at the university. He smoked and drank until the day when he couldn't light a cigarette or swallow a drink.

He studied at the university in the fifties and the Spanish poets Juan Ramón Jiménez and Pedro Salinas, who were his professors, expected everything of him. His first book of poems dates from that era, which appeared as a reprint from *La Torre*. It was the golden age of the university: a small and select student body, contentedly exiled professors from Europe or Latin America, the facility of teaching jobs just out of college and to study abroad, to return to the university with the honor of a degree. After a few years of lecturing on the basics, he managed to get sent to the Sorbonne. He wouldn't go to the Universidad Complutense in Madrid or to the Ivy League. He would make his way in a city where few Puerto Ricans ever arrived. At that time nobody had heard anything yet of the boom. On the island, anachronistically, Paris still suggested the times of Darío. But Esteves knew what he had in hand. He knew Vallejo and knew that behind Neruda, Lorca, and Alberti there were other texts, palimpsests written in French.

He spent four years in Europe. He made friends there but left little in the way of writing. He never wrote his thesis. He returned home with poetry that was passé. The legacy of Mallarmé, Apollinaire, and the surrealists didn't mix well with the poetry and battles of the socially conscious sixties. The university press published his only volume. He had few readers, and even they didn't really comprehend his wordplays, references, and lyricism.

He let more than twenty years go by between the university and La Torre bar, in an impoverished and bitter bohemia. His bimonthly salary check paid for the meals and drinking revelries of painters, poets, and singers who didn't have a penny to their name. There he became known to the next generation that practiced socially conscious poetry and defended other lyricisms. Among them he was obscure but not anonymous. There exist only two critical studies of his work, both by the most fanatical of the phonetic poets: this minimal attention attests to the failure of his literary life. His work was evaluated within a linguistic approach totally foreign to him.

Alejandro had been his student and, during his brief attempts to stop smoking, his supplier of cigarettes. As he did with me, Alejandro pestered him with his poems and with the desire to receive infinitely repeated applause.

I could think that Esteves's life had been a mistake if it weren't that he couldn't have had any other life. Poetry served no purpose anywhere, but trying to produce work responding to the avant-garde in a society where ignorance and pettiness killed everything: he could only fail. He had been a terse poet, perhaps minor, but this didn't matter. It was all the same, because here he couldn't be anything other than what he was. For him there was no possibility of another life, or another death.

The thought didn't escape me that all this was, in a way, a heavy-handed joke. Esteves was the living incarnation of characters I had invented in stories and a novel. I had imagined careers marked by excess and oblivion, sure that in some way they expressed the creator's destiny in a society like Puerto Rico. Now fate, if it existed, was making me face the reality of my fictions. Here was the writer whose life was the very proof of uselessness. What remained were his countless obscure publications, a considerable and fragile talent wasted in bars and sleepless nights, endless solitude, useless bitterness, and his pose of indifference. For Esteves, as for many others, the opportunity to be discovered posthumously did not exist. The hole in which he lived had been too big and what fell into it got lost. The effort of one man, or of a whole generation, did not suffice. He had before him an impossible task.

Alejandro called one day to ask me for a letter of recommendation. He was thinking of applying for a teaching job at the high school he'd left shortly before I met him, where he had studied until his junior year. I didn't think this was a good idea, especially not on my approval, but at his insistence I promised to do it.

There was still a lot of time before the start of the school year, and despite having gone through three interviews, they didn't promise him a decision until well into the summer. He looked elsewhere and ended up with a part-time job at a translation agency. I didn't hear from him for two or three weeks. I was sure that he must have been obsessively concentrating on his work. I knew that in his life any small matter or change was enough to capture his complete attention.

During that semester my first class was at seven in the morning. At around eight thirty, I'd usually end up in the faculty center to have a coffee and toast. Originally the center had been a kind of club for professors, but for many years it had deteriorated into a cafeteria serving the students. The piano, one room with armchairs and sofas, and the dining room reserved for the teachers, were all that were left of better times.

One morning I was surprised to run into Esteves. We went together to the counter. I ordered and saw that Esteves made a sign to the manager with his fingers. I was shocked to see them bring him a paper cup filled to the rim with a transparent liquid. "It's vodka," he explained. We went to sit at an empty table. At that hour there were very few people in the center. He drank and smoked with a repulsive resignation. We didn't speak. His attention was centered on the cup. He said goodbye with a nod, as if it didn't matter whether he did it or not, and I watched him walk toward the exit.

Shortly after this, I learned from a woman friend that the Spanish Department was considering suspending him. Perhaps this was inevitable and even the right thing to do, but I wondered how it would resolve anything. He had been forgotten for many years and no one seemed concerned about his being ill. Every once in a while, when I'd visit him, I found him suffering, submerged in a dreadful aura. I'd busy myself looking at the drawings and engravings of his friends, which he kept between two pieces of cardboard.

I'd observe him in his corner, tense, putting up with a pain that now nobody could relieve.

I wanted him to go to a doctor. I asked Alejandro to help me convince him. One day I found a message at the university:

Esteves was asking me to come see him. I had a brief moment of hope.

"I want you to listen to me without interrupting," he said just as I arrived. "I know what you do and why you do it. It's what I would have done for a friend. And I also want you to know this, that you are a friend and that I am sorry not to have time for your friendship. I am dying. I've known it for a year, since the doctor gave me three months to live. Now you can see how worthwhile prognoses are. I would have preferred to go quickly, because it's taken too long. It's hard when one knows one has nothing, not even time. Deep down, it's the same as before, but knowing it with certainty, with a time limit, is worse."

There was a pause; our eyes met.

"I don't want you to do anything. I don't want to go to the doctor or to the hospital. I simply want this to end. That's all. When the time comes, come here with Alejandro and take what you both want. Throw the rest out or leave it to the landlord. In the bank (I need you to do this, to find out how to have access to my account) there is money to dispose of me. Please, no wake or funeral: just bury me. That's all. I have no descendants, and I don't think my cousins really care to find out about me. Everything: books, papers, works of art, it's all yours. Take what you want. Throw the rest out."

"And if the moment arrives when you can no longer be here?"

"Then take me to the hospital. But to die only: no more examinations or doctors or tubes. My life ended some time ago; it's just that my body hasn't found out yet."

I left the apartment and went directly to look for Alejandro. As always he didn't want us to talk in his parents' house. We went to an awful pizzeria. I told him what I had talked about with Esteves. He thought it was impossible to follow his wishes to the letter. It was crazy to leave him alone in his apartment. Someone had to take charge. He had mentioned some family members. Perhaps we could contact them, or at least get someone to attend to him. I didn't expect such a response from him.

The next day Alejandro moved into his apartment. He could translate right there and I committed to bringing him and delivering his work and everything else that he needed. Esteves did not return to the university. Alejandro, who knew the Spanish Department professors, took charge of transmitting to them the news. Between the two of us we tried to make dying less cruel for him.

As the weeks passed, Alejandro became indispensable. He took charge of him day and night, kept him clean, and made the humiliation of the end bearable. His patience and good disposition to deal with the most intolerable chore were admirable. I never saw him more centered or close to a person. Never had the convolutions of his life seemed simpler.

We had to call an ambulance when Esteves fell into the stupor from which he never emerged. He lived six more days in a room in the general ward. According to his wishes, he was treated as little as possible. He died a little past four in the morning, with his skeletal hand in Alejandro's. I got to the hospital when the sun was coming up. I didn't know how to console Alejandro, who was in the bathroom, crying.

Two days later we buried him in the municipal cemetery. Besides Alejandro, my family, and myself, a retired professor wearing an absurd toupee was there. He couldn't resist the urge to smoke and to give a stuffy rhetorical speech about our national literature.

As we agreed, I took the boxes of books we didn't want to the Econolibros bookstore, which provided the commendable service of buying the libraries of dead people. I sent Alejandro the total sum from the sale, as well as the little more than a thousand dollars left in the bank account. From the apartment, he took some furniture, thinking that it would be useful for him when he moved from his parents' home. The rest—except for the works of art, in a very bad state of preservation, which we divided—remained in the apartment.

I stored in my workshop a cardboard box filled with hundreds of pages: Esteves's unpublished work and notes. A few days after his death, I opened it. The texts were not in order, his handwriting was difficult, and even the typed pages were filled with corrections made at different times. I knew that I couldn't edit them. The desolation in these pages was too much, that hopeless disorganized hoarding.

Early the next day, I called Alejandro and asked if we could meet at sunset at the Parque del Indio. In all the years we had known each other, I had almost never taken the initiative to get together with him. The death of Esteves had touched places I had not wanted to consider, and for the first time in a long time, I needed to talk, to try to tell someone what I was feeling. Life could end at any time, the demise of the poet made this clear, and it wasn't enough to try not to see reality, to live halfheartedly, protecting myself.

I found him sitting next to the fountain, facing the sea. As I approached, I remembered the conversations we had, with our backs to the cemetery, facing the blue wall of the nocturnal ocean and sky.

"It's a beautiful evening," he said.

"Yes, it's always lovely and those of us who live here barely realize it."

"It's as if the sea that surrounded us didn't exist."

"Yes, that's it," I said. "And yet, there is nothing more present than the sea that always circles us."

"Like a noose."

"Yes," I said, "like the noose around a hanged man's throat."

I called to the ice-cream vendor and asked for two cups of coconut. While we ate them I spoke again.

"I'm grateful to you for introducing me to Esteves."

"A good guy."

"He was, but he became something more than that for me. I saw his papers last night. It was enough to make one cry. I don't understand a thing, he must have pieces there from thirty or forty years back that he worked on and reworked without being able to produce a finished text."

"Enrique lost hope."

"One can see. Like many."

I watched him leave his ice cream unfinished and light a cigarette.

"I've thought a lot since his death," I said.

"What's there to think about? That's what awaits us. There's nothing more."

"Why do things have to be this way? I returned to Puerto Rico convinced that I would be able to do something. Esteves's death has made me see that my commitment has been basically half-assed. I've preferred to create a bunker: work, family, a routine, an exhibit here and there, a few books no one reads. But in reality I have never been happy and am afraid to face the bigger void that surrounds my little hole. So as not to see it, so as not to feel it, I've been willing, like Esteves, to drown myself, to leave behind a box of messy and useless papers. I am, after all, like many others: a career of frustration and isolation, a numbing habit of living from day to day. I have known how to hide it from myself for many years. I probably wouldn't have been able to stand this lucidity."

It was one of the few times, and the first in a long time, that Alejandro listened to me talking about myself. This wasn't totally his fault. I had preferred to let him express himself. I had complacently observed his madness because I was using it to protect myself, to feel out of danger. But I now realized there was no escape. The sea surrounded us. That was the most basic, ancient, and unwanted metaphor. I had to, I should, accept this fate. Nothing mattered as much as this. Not even being understood by Alejandro.

"Well, I don't know," said Alejandro. "I don't know what you're talking about."

"I'm talking about the sea," I said, convinced that I would never reach him and that this dialogue of deaf men was precisely my legacy, what we all have inherited, since the beginning of time. "No matter," I added, "it's logical that no one gets it: this is precisely the problem, fate, reality."

"I only know that Enrique died, that I'd like to move from my parents' house and get work at school; that I'm hungry; that there's no point; that I don't at all like such intellectualizing about suffering. That I want to get out of here."

He was such a son of a bitch. He'd always been—and would be until the day I decided it was not worth the trouble to ever see him again.

It was only on one of the many holidays in July that I once again had contact with him.

I had worked a lot, and as I had no expenses, I had saved the money with the intention of buying a car. Recently I had been presented with the opportunity of buying a Nissan Pathfinder in good condition despite its one hundred twenty thousand miles. As at home we were always short of cash, I thought of selling Alejandro the old Volkswagen Fox that we barely used now. The idea interested him and we agreed that he would come by to try it out. A few days later, we went out in the Fox with him at the steering wheel.

I had forgotten his driving: too fast, changing gears while trying to light a cigarette with a box of matches and the window opened. He'd turn suddenly at any corner, accelerate or stop short without any apparent logic. We took a long drive and, upon returning, the deal was done. A few days later I went to his house to make the transfer of the vehicle with a neighbor who was a lawyer. The living room was filled with dishes decorated with Spanish scenes, the center table and the shelves crammed with kitschy ceramics and figurines in terrible taste. Further inside, in the dark patio, one could imagine a profusion of hanging plants. It was a black hole of bad taste, like all that surrounded us in Puerto Rico to the point of tedium and disgust.

We went to the house of the lawyer who knew Alejandro since he was child. He treated him with a condescension that is often confused with responsibility and decency among adults. He asked me questions about the state of the car implying that he suspected deceit or cheating. Alejandro was getting more and more agitated until he devoted several minutes to a monologue in which he'd return endlessly to the same issues, trying, without any success, to reach a conclusion. The lawyer watched him with idiotic pity.

When we finished, I insisted that he take me home right away. I had no desire to be with him, even though I knew he wanted me to keep him company. I knew I was disappointing him but was not willing to watch him get lost in his labyrinths. Nor did I want him to force me to talk about his poems while he smoked and drank in a restaurant. It was useless to be with him.

Perhaps my refusal to linger that night displeased him, because weeks passed without his trying to contact me. Besides, the car probably made it possible for him to be more independent. Our relationship was always tenuous and I am sure that had anyone else been in his life, he would have preferred him.

During this period I saw him on the street several times and tried, without success, to attract his attention. He was driving or walking, distracted and alone. I even thought that he was pretending not to see me. I discovered him in the rearview mirror when I was driving around El Condado. I saw my former car and stuck my hand out the window, but almost immediately he changed lanes and passed me. On another occasion, he was walking along Roosevelt Avenue. He was probably leaving a pastry shop. The traffic was heavy that day and I didn't have time to signal to him. Another time I saw him on a side street in Ocean Park. His face and arms were red and he had a hard expression in his face. I pitied him, knowing that he was killing time. I knew the flavor of that solitude. I had lived it for so much longer than I had ever wanted.

One day, returning home from work, I found several messages from him on the answering machine. He wanted to see me as soon as possible, and that same night he came to pick me up. We went to the Middle Eastern restaurant where we had eaten many times. I listened to a hodgepodge impossible to follow, full of moments of uncertainty. He couldn't stand silence or the voice of anyone else. He didn't eat. He had ordered a beer, a coffee, and a package of cigarettes. In the end, I was left apprehensive.

He'd go to the Ocean Park beach at night to meet up with an Argentine man whom he knew almost nothing about except his name. He had asked him to bring a friend and the night before, when he was waiting for him by the sea, the man had appeared with two North American guys. They had hid among the sea grape that grew against the wall in front of the condominiums. He spoke of himself with a terrifying distance. I knew he wasn't lying.

The second piece of news was also peculiar. He had left his job at the translation agency. They had told him at the high school that they were probably firing a teacher and that they would use him to replace her. Alejandro took for certain this possibility and didn't want to have any commitments when they called him. He didn't realize he was playing with fire.

When he still hadn't finished dessert, he gave me an envelope with poems and insisted that I read them right then and there. I told him I couldn't, that a hasty reading would not do justice to his work. He got angry and drove me home. When he said good night, he informed me that he would call me the next day. It was a threat, a madman's call for help.

Around that time, I went out to take care of some chores and was still out when night fell. I didn't have to return immediately, so that I took a long ride around the city. I drove on without direction until I found myself on Kennedy Avenue going toward San Juan. I had Alejandro on my mind and remembered that I had always wanted to show him the lights on Constitution Bridge. Halfway down the avenue, there were only some faraway points of light, but as they advanced, the lines of poles rose until they created, for a few seconds, on each side of the road, immense question marks. It was one of the secret experiences of the city. I had showed it to a few friends, only to those who would understand its mystery and magic.

When I got home, I looked for the envelope he had given me and read his poems. They were the worst he had ever written: merely words placed aimlessly on the paper. I considered it useless to tell him this. He was sinking, and I could do nothing to help him. From the very beginning, our relationship had been stagnant and Alejandro had never had any warmth. I was one of the few players in his life. Nothing more. His part in my life, in turn, had been a way to build up my own. With my patience—if that's what it was—with him, I had tried to include in my hope that what I had lived in other cities had really existed. San Juan was something else. It was this. We were gossip and bad faith, good-natured contempt, rivals for jobs that didn't matter and that sometimes didn't even exist. I wasn't his friend, and didn't even get to be someone he respected. It was awful to see him, but for the first time in years, perhaps in my whole life, I didn't expect anything more. I was one step ahead. Free.

Some weeks later, he called. The position at the high school had not come through and this news, which he was shocked to receive, left him crushed. He didn't have the energy to look for another job. The only survival strategy he could come up with was to return to the university to audit a couple of courses. He'd spend the day at the seminar on Hispanic studies or in the library. Thus he amused himself and held onto a simulacrum of life.

One day he called, sounding so bad that I imagined how serious might his condition be when on the telephone, which had always been his most coherent form of communication, he could barely make himself understood. After lots of hemming and hawing, he asked me for a loan. I didn't object, but I couldn't see him just then and asked him to call me back in a few hours.

He did, two or three days later. Before repeating his request, he spoke at length. The sentences galloped along without order or transitions and I hadn't the slightest idea what he was saying or where he was heading with all this. At a given moment, he spoke to me of the poems he was working on and described to me a typography that formed visual images on the page. Just to say something, I mentioned Apollinaire. I was remembering an earlier conversation I had with him when he was still my student. Disconcerted, he repeated the poet's name and said that he didn't know him: that he knew of Rimbaud, Lautréamont, Breton, but that he had never heard of Apollinaire.

I thought he was pulling my leg. I reminded him of cubism and the surrealists; I alluded to our past conversation and I eventually realized that there was no humor or irony in his words. Something unfathomable was happening. Emotion took me by the throat. Alejandro was one more shipwreck, another of an endless series, collapsing within the boundaries of silence on this island. I had known many; I had come very close to being one of them.

Confused, I listened to how he proposed to sell me the car. He wanted to know if I was interested in buying it back for a third of the price he had paid me for it. He had crashed into a pole (on Kennedy Avenue no less) and the car couldn't run now. He said I could use it for parts or try to fix it. I promised to let him know if I knew of anyone who was interested. In the end, he asked again for some money. I made a date with him the following day at the university.

Very early I saw him peeking inside the door to my office. I invited him to come in and sit for a while, but he refused because he was smoking. Smoking was prohibited in that area of small offices without windows. I suggested that he put out the cigarette, but he preferred to remain in the doorway, only half his body visible while he kept his hand as far away as possible and, from time to time, took quick puffs. I knew how he felt, what it's like to give up the chance of a crucial conversation for a few inches of tobacco. His priorities were clear. It was also the only pleasure he had left.

In answer to my question, he said that things were bad, that he wanted to sell the car to return to New York and look for work. I realized that he was too anxious to want to talk. I asked him to keep me posted, that before doing anything, he should call or come see me. I knew he wouldn't. Without looking at me, he asked if I could give him ten more pesos to buy a book. I took out the money and gave it to him in the doorway. He put the butt in his mouth and shook my hand as if I were a stranger.

Maybe telling his story is as useless as trying to forget it. But it doesn't matter anymore because I have these pages. I'm still here, continuing to write the ending that was always there from the beginning, finding in Alejandro the path that was also mine. It would have been enough to write: "Here his story ends. Here silence begins." But this is not true because Alejandro must be somewhere, and if he reads this someday, perhaps it won't be bad for him to discover the efforts, the pain, and the failure of generations.

The sea stretches like a desert around the city and the island; the sea is there to drown in. I can say that I am almost happy to come to this realization. Finally this land is mine.

San Juan, 2001–2003